C000156246

Rosie, Where are You?

Tales of a Twenty-First Century Housekeeper

ROSEMARY E KEELE

2QT (Publishing) Ltd

First Edition published 2019 by

2QT Limited (Publishing)
Settle, North Yorkshire BD24 9RH United Kingdom

Printed by Ingram Sparks

Front cover images: Shutterstock.com
Other images: Shutterstock.com & Vecteezy.com

A CIP catalogue record for this book is available from the British Library

ISBN - 978-1-913071-01-1

Introduction

When I tell people I am a retired Housekeeper the assumption is that I worked in an hotel. When I explain that I worked in various stately homes for the, usually titled, owners I am met with expressions of surprise that such places still exist in the twenty-first century. Not only do they exist but a lot of them are thriving through using the main family asset, the ancestral pile, as a means of earning a crust.

This means that the modern role of Housekeeper is a diverse and busy role. Today a good Housekeeper will take on many roles. As a cook she can rustle up anything from a simple loaf of bread to a grand four or five course supper for 20. As a lady's maid she can remove stains from any garment, mend any tear, launder any fabric and foresee every need of her employer. As a housemaid she must look after the day-to-day cleaning of carpets and polishing of furniture, glass, brass and silver. As a scullery-maid she must keep the kitchen table, floors, cupboards and appliances scrubbed and the pots, pans, crockery and cutlery clean. As the butler she must be discreet, selectively deaf and at the same time be able to respond to any request positively and immediately. She must be able to adapt to any role required of her and always be available, day or night, forever tireless, emotionless and without complaint.

I have decided to write these stories in response to many requests received over the years that I document my experiences. However, the house, the family, the village and the dale in these stories does not exist. None of the events described in the stories happened though I have used my many happy memories as a catalyst to produce them. Even in retirement discretion must be maintained.

Rosemary E. Keele.

Contents

The Flower Arrangements

'Rosie! Rosie! Where are you?'

Lady Linton's shrill voice could be heard ringing around the ground floor of Threldale Hall. She was the sort of woman you invariably heard before you saw, and today was no exception. Normally I would not see or hear from her until after she had breakfasted unless I was in trouble, and I did my best to make sure that did not happen. So it was a little unusual to hear her calling for me from the Entrance Hall as soon as she came down, before even going into the Dining Room.

I decided to ignore it for now and hoped I would have peace for a few more precious moments in the warmth and comfort of the Kitchen. This was one room where I was usually left alone. The Kitchen was a spacious room with two large but high windows (no point having windows the servants could idle away their time looking out of), two big Belfast sinks under the windows, a big scrubbed pine table in the middle of the floor, a modern Aga where the coal-fired range used to be and an electric range cooker.

There were floor-to-ceiling cupboards along the full length of the wall opposite the windows and what had once been a scullery off to the side. This was now used by me as a pantry. To get to the Kitchen from the house you went through a door just to one side of the main staircase into what was once the servants' passage. There were other rooms that could be accessed along this passage, but the first of these was the Kitchen. This meant that, should she call me, I would be able to easily hear Lady Linton.

As housekeeper at Threldale peace was usually in short supply, and I cherished the few moments that I did manage to get. Lady Linton could be quite a demanding person to work for at the best of times. She had very high expectations regarding my capabilities – somewhere between Wonder Woman and Superwoman.

As for the amount of help I had on a day-to-day basis to run the hall … the number of staff working inside Threldale itself was greater than zero but less than two. As a consequence my days as housekeeper cum cook cum general dogsbody were long, starting early in the morning, often finishing late in the evening, and every moment full to bursting with things to do. Not only was I never idle but I was never bored either.

This was not a nine-to-five job with weekends off and six weeks' paid holiday each year. This was a way of life. I had my own little flat on the top floor, converted from four of the eight old servants' bedrooms of days gone by, with views across the front lawns to the hills beyond. It consisted of a sitting room, a bathroom and two bedrooms. I did all my cooking using the main Kitchen downstairs. This flat came free with the job: no rent to pay, no rates, and all the logs I could burn in the open fire in my small but cosy sitting room. Not a bad perk, but it did mean that I was at the beck and call of Lady Linton at all times. She was not above knocking on my flat door on my day off with some emergency that could not wait until I was back on duty.

I was not totally on my own during the years I worked for the Linton family. There were two gardeners, Sam and Don, but our duties did not overlap. They were kept on their toes raising vegetables in the walled garden for me to use in the Kitchen, keeping the lawns at the front of the Threldale Hall in order and doing odd jobs around the estate. They rarely came into the house, and if they did it was by the side door and it would only be as far as the Kitchen. They tried to keep their heads down and stay out of the way of Lady Linton as much as they could – something I would have liked to have done too, but that was not an option that was available to me.

Back inside Threldale, I had been up and working since 7 a.m. and it was now 10 a.m. The drawing room, the Library and the Entrance Hall had been dusted, swept and wiped. The cushions had been plumped, the bins emptied and other rubbish had been removed, and everywhere had been generally tidied up. I was not allowed to vacuum until everyone was downstairs for breakfast. I had cleaned and tidied the Dining Room from supper the previous evening, set the table for breakfast, made the bread for the day, squeezed the oranges, cooked the bacon, scrambled the eggs and made the porridge. That just left the toast and a pot of coffee, both of which would have to be freshly made once Lord and Lady Linton arrived in the Dining Room ready to have their breakfast. The morning papers had been delivered and I had left them on the dining table ready to be perused and discussed over the toast and coffee.

On a day-to-day basis I had very few dealings with Lord Linton. He tended to be either out and about on the estate with Sam and Don pointing out jobs to do, or in the Library, which doubled up as his office and from where he dealt with the day-to-day running of the Threldale estate. However, the same could not be said of my dealings with Lady Linton. I never knew from day to day whether she would be in a relaxed mood, and therefore I could get on with my planned chores, of which there were many, or in a demanding mood, and I would have to throw out any plans I had for the day in favour of whatever it was she had on her mind. Today looked like being one of those demanding days.

'Rosie! Rosie! Where are you?' Lady Linton's voice was a little louder, and it shrilled. She was not going to be ignored. I was going to have to go and find out what it was she wanted.

'Just coming, Lady Linton,' I shouted, untying and removing my apron before leaving the Kitchen to go and present myself in person in the Dining Room and find out what it was Lady Linton wanted.

'There you are. Didn't you hear me calling? Really, you need to pay more attention and stop idling your time away hiding in corners. I shouldn't have to keep repeating myself all the time.' Lady Linton was sitting down at the dining table with a glass of orange juice, a bowl of porridge and the morning paper propped up against the marmalade pot.

'Sorry, Lady Linton.' I had learnt many years ago that it was easier to apologise for any perceived misdemeanour, regardless of whether I was guilty or not.

'I have decided that the rooms look a little bare and unwelcoming. It is high time that Threldale had a bit of colour. I want flower arrangements in all the reception rooms downstairs and in my rooms upstairs.' This was something she had not asked for before.

'Yes, Lady Linton.'

'Except the Library, of course. Lord Linton can't abide anything in there that may damage his precious books or get in the way of whatever it is he does in there.'

'No, Lady Linton.'

'Not formal, showy displays. I can't stand stand anything arty or artificial when it comes to flowers. Keep it organic, green and natural.'

'Yes, Lady Linton.'

'No fancy ribbons or other fussiness. No gaudy colours or bits of plastic. Just simple flower arrangements in nice vases. We do have plenty of vases, don't we?'

'Yes, Lady Linton.'

'I want them done this morning. I am sure you will have time. Lord Linton and I have no plans that should disturb you – apart from lunch, that is – and I am sure you aren't overwhelmed with work. We aren't expecting anyone today.'

I had actually planned to valet the bedrooms, wash, dry and iron today's laundry, sort out and repair the bed linen, polish the household silver, start cleaning the inside of the windows, get the dirty marks off the paintwork in the Entrance Hall, and all in between providing meals and refreshments as and when required for Lord Linton and Lady Linton. So, while I wasn't overwhelmed, I was busy.

'Yes, Lady Linton.' So much for my planned workload. I would have to reprioritise everything and put the flower arrangements at the top.

'Well, don't just stand there dawdling. I expect to see the results of your labours by lunchtime.'

'Very good, Lady Linton.'

End of conversation. I made some fresh toast and a pot of coffee, popped them on the table in the Dining Room and retreated to my sanctuary in the Kitchen. Now that everything was ready in the Dining Room I could sit down for a few moments and give some thought to my new duty of sorting out flower arrangements.

Hopefully, I would now have a couple of hours to get something organised before returning to the chores I had originally planned for the day. How many do I need to do? How big do they need to be? What should I put in them? These were questions that I could not ask Lady Linton. She expected her wishes to be carried out without her having to answer what

12

she saw as unnecessary questions. I should be able to read her mind. So this was a new skill I was going to have to learn, and learn quickly, on my own, with absolutely no idea where to begin.

Lady Linton had never expressed a desire for displays before, and there was no money left in the household budget for that week for me to be able to buy such extras. And, even if there had been, I didn't have time to nip out and buy flowers. The beautiful but obscure dale that Threldale Hall sat in was quite isolated, and the nearest place where I would be able to buy anything from was an hour's drive away. I knew from experience that lack of money and time would not be seen as acceptable excuses for the failure to produce the arrangements as requested. Lady Linton had decreed that there would be flowers, artistically arranged in vases and in place by lunchtime, and that was what she expected to see.

I donned my coat, grabbed a couple of baskets, a pair of secateurs and a knife from the garden room, took the keys to the battered old golf buggy (this was used to access the furthest corners of the estate) from the secure key cupboard in the Entrance Hall, walked around to the garage, hopped into the buggy and drove off across the lawns to the wilder parts of the estate looking for inspiration. It was a cold spring day but at least it wasn't raining or blowing a gale. Both were a common occurrence in this part of the world.

Threldale Hall was nestled in the bottom of the dale, which meant that the views around the estate were stunning: grand hills with craggy slopes covered in bracken and purple heather. I was going to make the most of this time out in the fresh air looking at the views across the dale and the farms on the hillsides. A mile or so from the gates to the estate was the village of Hargrove, the only other place of any size in the dale but not visible from from the grounds.

The estate was full of late spring colour. Most of it was wild flowers – none of which, I am ashamed to say, I had any names for, beyond the easily recognisable ones such as daisies, buttercups and dandelions. I just hoped none of the ones I didn't recognise were rare species that I was about to destroy by chopping off their blooms. I started snipping away at some of the taller stemmed flowers that looked colourful – to me, anyway – and the first basket was soon filled with blooms. Now I needed lots of greenery to balance it all out.

There was quite a range of shrubs and bushes on the estate, and most of them were large, overgrown and very green, so it was only a matter of minutes before I had the second basket full. My hands were scratched and dirty but I felt quite pleased with my collection. I was quite warm with my exertions, but it was time to head back to Threldale to exercise my non-existing artistic skill at organic flower arranging.

I parked the estate buggy back in the garage where I borrowed it from, put the keys back in the key cupboard and carried my baskets down past the Kitchen, along the corridor and into the garden room, so called because once upon a time anything coming in from the garden was put in this room. I put the two baskets on the old wooden table, went to one of the old cupboards, retrieved a selection of differing sizes of vases, set them out on the table, emptied the two baskets and set to work with the flowers and greenery.

An hour later I had what I thought was quite a selection of passable flower arrangements in an assortment of vases. There were enough to put at least a couple in each of the reception rooms. I stepped back and admired my handiwork. The floor and the table of the garden room were covered in discarded clippings that I would clear up later, but for now the flower arrangements were ready.

I took the flower arrangements in their vases out one at a time and placed my handiwork on various tables in the Dining Room, the Entrance Hall, the drawing room and Lady Linton's dressing room and bedroom. I did not put anything in any of the rooms in Lord Linton's bedroom suite as I did not think he would appreciate the gesture. There were other rooms downstairs, but they were closed up and not used. Feeling very pleased with myself, I returned to the Kitchen to restart my day. It was half past twelve and time to set my mind to what to prepare for lunch.

Later, and just half an hour into lunch preparations, my routine was shattered.

'Rosie! Rosie! Where are you?' Lady Linton sounded loud and impatient. 'Rosie! Rosie! Are you there?' she shouted in the general direction of the Kitchen.

'Just coming, Lady Linton,' I called, removing my

15

apron, wiping my hands and heading in the direction of Lady Linton's summoning call. I hoped whatever it was that she wanted me for it would not take too long or lunch would not be ready at 1 30 p.m. as planned, and Lord Linton did not like his lunch to be late.

'There you are,' she said as I arrived in the Entrance Hall, where she stood waiting for me with her hands on her hips. ' These flowers ... where did you get them from?'

'The estate grounds, Lady Linton.' I sensed trouble coming my way.

'Do you mean wild flowers?' she said, rather sharply.

'Yes, Lady Linton.'

'Not from some hidden flower bed somewhere on the estate?'

'No, Lady Linton. There are no flower beds any more. The gardeners grassed them over last year.'

'I know, I know. I haven't forgotten. The gardeners don't have time to shilly-shally with flower beds when the vegetable garden is a much more productive proposition for Threldale's needs. So the flowers were not purchased?'

'No, sorry. I didn't have time to go out to a florist and purchase any flowers. Besides, there wasn't anything left in the household budget for this week, Lady Linton.' I was pushing my luck by coming out with meaningless excuses.

'You mean you picked wild flowers from the estate grounds?'

'Yes, Lady Linton.'

'Well, I would have thought someone of your years

16

of experience would know not to pick wild flowers. Some of them might be rare specimens. In future, when putting together flower arrangements, you do not pick any wild flowers of any description. As you have already produced these flower arrangements, they will have to do, but in future do not, I repeat, do *not* pick wild flowers!' Lady Linton gave me a stern look, turned and headed for the drawing room, leaving me standing alone in the hall.

Well, that was me well and truly put in my place. I retreated back to the peace of the Kitchen and continued with preparations for lunch, and put anything to do with flower arrangements to the back of my mind. There was nothing I could do until I had to replace the existing ones with fresh ones in a couple of weeks' time. No more was said, but I knew from experience that Lady Linton had not finished with the subject.

A couple of weeks later I made sure the regular delivery of groceries from the local supermarket to Threldale included a selection of cut flowers – cheap cut flowers. They were very cheap, but were still simple and colourful flowers. Spread out over the same vases, with lots of architectural greenery, there should be just enough to go round.

I set off around the estate grounds in the buggy and collected lots of greenery from the various shrubs and bushes on the estate, and again I set to in the garden room turning the cheap supermarket flowers and estate greenery into simple flower arrangements.

Once more I was quite pleased with my efforts. The mixture of greenery and flowers looked organic and natural, as requested. I placed my efforts in the same rooms on the same tables as my previous attempts of a couple of weeks earlier and waited, with some trepidation, for the verdict from Lady Linton.

The rest of the morning passed quietly without sight or sound of Lady Linton to interrupt my routine. She was scarily quiet. I would much rather she sought me out and told me, good or bad, what she thought of the flower arrangements. Hearing nothing was far too stressful. Previous experience had taught me that silence was not a good sign.

There were guests, friends of Lady Linton, arriving for lunch, so I was busy cleaning rooms, preparing food and setting the Dining Room up ready, while Lady Linton spent the time dealing with correspondence and preparing herself for her guests. Such are the trials and tribulations of a lady and her housekeeper.

The guests were due to arrive for pre-lunch drinks at twelve thirty, so I made sure everything was ready and awaiting their arrival at that time. Canapés: check. Chilled wine: check. Clean, smear-free glasses: check. Soft drinks option: check.

Lunch was a simple quiche with a mixed green salad and a caprese salad (an Italian dish of tomatoes, basil and mozzarella dressed with olive oil and seasoning), with a fruit salad to follow afterwards. This meant that the various dishes just needed putting on the sideboard in the Dining Room, from where Lady Linton and her guests could then help themselves when they were ready to lunch. By this time I was starting to think that maybe – just maybe – this time the flower arrangements were going to pass muster.

At one thirty the doorbell rang. They were only an hour late. Not bad. I have known guests arrive many hours later than expected, not turn up, or even arrive on the wrong day. I have also known more guests arrive than catered for, as well as fewer guests. I have learnt over the years to always ensure the food would stretch to at least one extra mouth and would not spoil if lunch was late.

I removed my apron, left the Kitchen and headed out into the Entrance Hall and towards the front door. Before I had got halfway across the hall I was intercepted by Lady Linton coming out of the drawing room.

'Ah, Rosie, I will get the door. I am sure you have lots to get on with.'

'Yes, Lady Linton.'

I turned round and went back through the door to the passage that led to the Kitchen, there I hovered out of view. Previous lunches and suppers had taught me not to wander off too far when there were guests in the house. More often than not I would find that my services were required despite being dismissed. From my vantage point I could clearly hear Lady Linton's voice as she welcomed her friends to Threldale Hall.

'Hello, Constance. Lovely to see you.

'Amelia, you look well.

'Beatrice, welcome. Come in.

'Oh, the flowers. Yes, they are lovely, aren't they?

19

'Yes, they were freshly done this morning.

'Thank you. So glad you like them.

'No, Rosie is far too busy, so I do them as my small contribution to the smooth running of the house. It gives me a chance to show my artistic side. Yes, it does take time but one must make sacrifices if one is to keep staff these days.

'They are rather green and organic, aren't they? I much prefer the natural look.'

The cheek of the woman! Taking all the credit for my hard work. It took a lot of my self-control not to splutter behind the door during this exchange. I would never hear the end of it if Lady Linton thought I had been eavesdropping on her conversations. I should have known. After all, I was only the housekeeper at Threldale Hall. At least I was now sure that the flower arrangements met with Lady Linton's approval, even if I had used the least expensive ones available from the supermarket.

The WI Tour

From my vantage point behind the door in the Kitchen passage I could see Lord and Lady Linton striding into the entrance of Threldale Hall after attending the Sunday morning service at St Luke's Anglican church in Hargrove village. Lord Linton did not look happy. In fact he looked decidedly out of sorts. He tended to be a little bit taciturn at the best of times but the look on his face as he came into the house was beyond taciturn, past tetchy and well into grumpy. Something must have happened while they were at church because he had been quite happy when he left to walk to Hargrove an hour and a half ago.

The majority of the buildings in the village were still owned by the Lintons, despite the passing of several generations. They also still owned a large proportion of the surrounding fields, forest and farms. As both the hall and the village were situated off the beaten track in one of the more obscure dales in Yorkshire it was a quiet place to live, if a little isolated and feudal in its outlook.

Not much tourist traffic made it into Hargrove unless people had got lost looking for one of the more well-known dales and needed directions on how to get out of our little dale again. The stream running through the bottom of the dale was pretty but not picturesque. There were no spectacular waterfalls, known potholes, or coarse fishing. The hills climbing up the sides of the dale were not high enough or rugged enough to attract the hardy walkers, and the bracken and heather that crowned them was not of any special scientific interest. The wildlife consisted of lots of rabbits, flocks of crows and the odd buzzard.

There was still a lot of respect in the village for those who lived up at the hall, and the villagers liked to see that Lord and Lady Linton still attended the Sunday services at the church and took an active interest in village life. They would often stop and chat to people after the service, catching up on the births, marriages, illnesses and deaths in the old families who had lived in the dale for generations.

They would discuss farming matters with the hill farmers, such as livestock purchases, sales or new arrivals, and maybe the acquisition of new or second-hand machinery, the state of the spring grass or the march of bracken down the hillside. After due attention had been paid to the residents of the farms and the village they would walk back to Threldale Hall for a well-earned Sunday lunch, and this Sunday had been no exception.

Lady Linton removed her hat, unbuttoned her coat and put her handbag on the hall table before turning to Lord Linton.

'You should have said no. It isn't as if you know anything about the WI.' It sounded as though Lord

Linton had agreed to something to do with the WI that he shouldn't have. He had a history of agreeing to things that he shouldn't if he felt cornered.

'I couldn't get away from the damn woman pestering me for an answer. I couldn't push past her to leave the church without being rude. I had to agree to do it before she would let me pass. You will have to deal with it. I have no patience with chattering women, especially that woman. She is the most unpleasant person I have ever met,' snapped Lord Linton. He stomped off towards the Library to try and wind down before lunch.

'Well, the deed is done now. I will speak to Rosie. I am sure she will be more than capable of taking it off your hands,' Lady Linton called after him as he shut the Library door behind him. She turned away and headed towards the door to the Kitchen passage, presumably to ask me to take whatever it was off Lord Linton's hands.

I decided to head her off and came out through the passage door to meet her.

'Ah, Rosie. Do you know anything about the Hargrove WI?' she enquired.

'No, Lady Linton,' I replied. I had no idea what Lord Linton had agreed to do for the Hargrove WI, but I was sure it meant more work for me. However, like him, I knew nothing about the WI and had never even been to a WI meeting.

'Well, Mrs Waltroyd is their president and she very rudely cornered Lord Linton after church this morning and she has persuaded him – or maybe I should say bullied – into giving the WI a tour of Threldale Hall and a talk about the Linton family history,' she explained. 'He has no idea how much is involved in organising something like this. He really should have said no. I can't understand why he agreed to it.'

'Yes, Lady Linton.' I was not going to volunteer for anything. I would wait until I had no choice but to take on whatever was coming my way.

'It means we have a bit of a problem. Now that Lord Linton has been somewhat bulldozed into making a promise to Mrs Waltroyd, we must be seen to act on it. I think he honestly believed it was the only way he could get away from the woman. So there will have to be a tour and a talk, but there is no way he will do it. He finds her most tedious, and the thought of talking to a whole group of women who she is president of will have him running for the hills,' she continued, looking at me to make sure I was paying attention.

'Yes, Lady Linton.' I was still giving nothing away.

'I am far too busy over the next few weeks to organise something like this. You know all about the history of Threldale Hall and the Linton family. I am sure I can trust you to step in and deal with Mrs Waltroyd and the Hargrove WI. Just keep me informed of the details.'

'Yes, Lady Linton.' So I was to pick the problem up.

Having passed the hornets' nest on to me Lady Linton disappeared upstairs to her rooms to change for lunch, leaving me standing in the Entrance Hall trying not to look gobsmacked. I had never given a talk to any group on any subject at any time in my life. I'm a housekeeper, not a tour guide. As for my knowledge of Threldale Hall and the Linton family history … well, that was a bit weak, to say the least. It was no good me arguing or coming up with excuses. Lady Linton had spoken. There would be a tour and a talk on Threldale Hall and the Linton family history given to the ladies of the Hargrove WI by me.

Before I could do anything I needed to speak to this Mrs Waltroyd, the woman who had upset Lord Linton so much. First thing the next morning I telephoned her in her capacity as the president of the Hargrove WI, to get the ball rolling. As it would be early afternoon before I would have completed my chores and cleared away lunch I invited her to come up to Threldale for a coffee around the middle of the afternoon, leaving the exact timing down to her, and this she readily agreed to do.

So far she didn't sound like the pushy woman Lord Linton disliked so much, and so I started hoping that this might be an easier task than I had first thought. I asked her to come to the side door rather than the front door. I didn't tell her why, but I didn't want her bumping into Lord or Lady Linton. She might think she was going to be talking to them instead of me. I would let her in and we would settle ourselves down in the cosy warmth of the Kitchen to discuss the details. It also meant I could get things organised my way without interference from Lady Linton or upsetting Lord Linton.

I spent the rest of the morning and the first part

of the afternoon serving breakfast, valeting rooms, sorting out the laundry and preparing, serving and clearing away lunch.

At precisely 3 p.m. there was a sharp rat-a-tat at the side door. Barely had I opened the door than Mrs Waltroyd pushed in past me without introducing herself, which I thought was rather rude of her. I would have to revise my opinion of her if she continued in that manner.

'Where do you want me?' she asked, fixing me with a questioning look.

'Follow me, please. We are going into the first room on the right, the Kitchen. We will make ourselves comfortable in there while we discuss the arrangements,' I said, brushing past her to get into the Kitchen first and heading for the Aga to make the coffee. This was my domain and I would not have this woman waltzing in like she owned the place. My first impression of her was changing fast. Now she was here she came across as bossy and domineering. No wonder Lord Linton was not impressed by her.

'Very good of you to organise this for the Hargrove WI. Just the sort of thing our ladies are interested in. Lots of information on the local family seat, something they can relate to. The families of a lot of our ladies have lived in the same house in Hargrove or on the same farm in the dale for generations. I already see this being a bit of a feather in our WI cap. If my ladies find it interesting we could pass word around other WIs in the area. You may find others wanting to come for a tour of Threldale. Capital! Now shall we get started?' she enthused, barely drawing breath between sentences.

I couldn't see Lord or Lady Linton agreeing to further tours for other WI groups. In fact I couldn't see them agreeing to other tours for any groups. They weren't happy about this one. I put on a fixed smile as I put the coffee jug on a tray with cups and saucers and a plate of home-made biscuits, took them over to the Kitchen table and settled down with Mrs Waltroyd to discuss the WI tour details.

The next twenty minutes were taken up with discussing possible dates and times, duration and refreshments. She also wanted to know how much Lord and Lady Linton would be involved with the tour and talk. I nipped that one in the bud by stating that I would be running the visit. Most of the rest came as demands on her part rather than requests for her ladies. I would like to say that we mutually agreed the details but it was more a case of me agreeing to what Mrs Waltroyd dictated, with little or no room for discussion.

By the end of our discussions I felt as if I had been verbally mugged. We put the information in our respective diaries and moved on to more general conversation. I would have hoped to have been able to say it was a relaxed and easy-going conversation, but I felt as though I was being quizzed by some policeman for information relating to a crime.

'Do you run this house on your own?' she enquired.
'Yes, I do.'

'Both Lord and Lady Linton seem a lovely couple, and such an asset to Hargrove and our lovely dale. Don't you agree?

'Of course.' I tried not to give anything away.

'You must like working for them in such a wonderful house.' She really was a nosy woman.

'Yes, this is their home and I just happen to run it for them.'

'That must be difficult. Threldale Hall is so large. Do you get much time off?' She was definitely fishing for gossip.

'I manage to get the time off that I am entitled to have.' This woman was really starting to annoy me with her prying questions.

'That sounds like you are trying to be tactful.'

What did she expect me to say?

'Not at all. I love working here. It is more a way of life than a job.'

'Is it much different, do you think, to how it was, say, fifty years ago?'

I'd had enough. Mrs Waltroyd had pushed her questions beyond the limits of confidentiality. I was not sure how far or how much to say to someone I hardly knew, much less someone I didn't like, and I decided to stop it there.

'I must get on, Mrs Waltroyd. I will confirm the arrangements we have made with Lady Linton.' I said, closing the conversation down as politely as I could.

'Certainly, certainly. I must move on too. Lots to do. You have no idea how much is involved in running the Hargrove WI. I look forward to the day of the tour. I am sure it will be a great success. The ladies would have preferred either Lord or Lady Linton hosting the tour, but I quite understand they are busy people.'

And with that she finished her coffee, gathered her belongings and left the hall by the same way she had come in. Whether I liked my job or not was none of this woman's business.

I made Lady Linton aware of the date and time the Hargrove WI would be coming and explained that Mrs Waltroyd had requested tea and biscuits for her ladies after the tour and talk.

'Good. I knew you would be able to organise this, Rosie. It all sounds very reasonable. I will join the group for refreshments in the drawing room, but I doubt Lord Linton will want to put in an appearance. I suspect he will keep to the Library for the duration of the visit. I will leave you to get on with it.'

Over the next few days I made lots of notes about what I should say in my talk. Lord Linton was happy to give me some guidance and lots of information, which was not surprising, as he didn't have to deliver the talk. Maybe he was feeling guilty that I had to pick this up on his behalf, and that thanks to me he was not having to deal with the awful Mrs Waltroyd.

I gave a lot of thought to what to show them as regards the rooms they would be allowed access to. At Threldale not all the rooms were furnished with items of historical interest. Some of them were very modern, and some of them were so mundane that they were quite boring. Some rooms were very private and personal. Some had not been used by Lord and Lady Linton for many years, and as a result were in a state of neglect and disrepair. Two rooms that were in this sorry state were the Orangery and the Morning Room, so they would be out of bounds. Once I had a list of rooms to take the WI ladies around I sought Lady Linton's approval for my selection.

Early on the day of the tour Lord Linton was already up, and he soon left to spend the day at York Races with friends rather than stay at Threldale and risk bumping into the ladies of the Hargrove WI, Mrs Waltroyd in particular. He took great delight in informing Lady Linton that he would be lunching out and would not be back until that evening.

Lady Linton took an equal delight in informing me that she was going into the Library, now that Lord Linton was going to be out for the day (this room was one that the WI ladies would not be allowed access to). She indicated that she had pressing correspondence to catch up on and she was not to be disturbed for any reason. She would join the Hargrove WI in the drawing room, as previously arranged, for tea at the end of the tour. I think they were both avoiding Mrs Waltroyd in their different ways. I wished I could avoid her as well.

Once I had done all my usual chores I was able to spend the rest of the morning baking cakes and biscuits, setting up cups and saucers and readying the drawing room for the visitors. I wandered around the various rooms running through the tour in my head one last time. During our discussions Mrs Waltroyd had told me there were thirty-two members in the Hargrove WI, but she only expected about eighteen to attend on the day.

By the time the WI ladies arrived I was relaxed and ready to deliver my talk on the Linton family history and show them round certain parts of Threldale Hall, which I had agreed with Lady Linton beforehand. She had been very insistent that the ladies where not taken into any additional rooms over and above those agreed. As they filed in through the front door I counted fifteen ladies altogether, including Mrs Waltroyd, a number I could easily cope with.

Off we went, starting in the Entrance Hall and then moving around the ground floor to the drawing room, the Dining Room and the unused and unloved billiard room. I pointed out key family portraits, items of antique furniture, delicate pieces of porcelain and handwoven carpets in the different rooms. I took the ladies upstairs to show them two of the rooms used for guests, the Chinese bedroom, with its beautiful hand-painted four-poster bed and original imported Chinese wallpaper, and the blue bedroom. The private bedroom suites of Lord and Lady Linton were off limits. The tour finished off with the Kitchen passage to the service rooms and the cellar (where the laundry room was), the garden room and my domain, the Kitchen, all of which seemed to interest the ladies more than the grander family rooms in the main part of the house.

Once I had finished the tour of Threldale I steered the ladies back towards the drawing room, opened the door and ushered them inside. Lady Linton, having finished her pressing correspondence in the Library, was already there, waiting for them to come in. She came forward to introduce herself to the ladies and proceeded to make them feel at home, something she could do with ease when she wanted to. I left them chatting with her while I went back to the Kitchen to make the tea and coffee. The cakes and biscuits were already on serving plates on one of the butler's tables I had set up for the purpose. Another butler's table held the tray of cups and saucers and sugar and milk.

On my return, with the pots of freshly made tea and coffee, I could see that Mrs Waltroyd had cornered Lady Linton over by one of the windows. The other ladies were standing about in small groups smiling and discussing the tour and what they had seen. I set about pouring teas and coffees for the ladies and telling them to help themselves to the cakes and biscuits, while keeping one ear on the conversation by the window. I could hear Mrs Waltroyd's voice carrying clearly across the room.

'Marvellous tour, Lady Linton. That housekeeper of yours is very informative about the family portraits, the various antiques and whatnots you have. Certainly knows how give an interesting talk and how to keep the WI ladies interested. As I told her, when I called to arrange details, if my ladies enjoy the tour we shall pass on your details to other WIs in the dales.' Mrs Waltroyd was in full flow.

'I am so glad you enjoyed it but it was just a one-off,' smiled Lady Linton a little abstractedly. I think she was finding Mrs Waltroyd hard work. 'Lord Linton sends his apologies. He had a meeting to attend elsewhere, otherwise he would have been here himself to welcome you. He is so sorry to have missed you,' she continued.

'What's her name again? It's just slipped my mind.' Mrs Waltroyd ploughed on, choosing not to hear or just plain ignoring whatever Lady Linton had just said.

'Rosie. Her name is Rosie,' said Lady Linton, nonplussed at the slight.

'Yes, that's right. Don't know how she does it. She must be an absolute godsend, looking after this place for you. I never got the chance to ask her... Does she live in? I suppose she must, given her erratic hours. Such a big house. There must be a lot for her to do every day.' I had a terrible sense of dread as she continued, barely pausing to draw breath. I could hardly bear to listen.

'Had a cosy chat with her in the Kitchen the day we sorted out the details for tour. She is a very busy lady. I believe she does all the day-to-day jobs around Threldale Hall. It's so hard these days, trying to find anyone prepared to work as hard as she does. With so much to do, she must get very little time to herself. I would give my right arm to find daily help on a par with your housekeeper. I was surprised to know she ran this beautiful house on her own.' Mrs Waltroyd just prattled on, regardless of any gaffes she might be making while Lady Linton stared at her in utter disbelief.

'On her own! I think you will find that Rosie helps me to run this house!' She was quite dumbfounded at Mrs Waltroyd's faux pas.

'I say, Lady Linton, I didn't mean to offend. I do apologise,' spluttered Mrs Waltroyd.

'I should think so! I must go and talk to my other guests. I am sure you can entertain yourself,' Lady Linton snapped. She excused herself and strode off to talk to some of the other ladies. Mrs Waltroyd was left standing by the window looking rather embarrassed.

I had a funny feeling that trouble, in the form of an outraged Lady Linton, would be heading my way once the WI ladies had left, all thanks to the ignorant Mrs Waltroyd. She had obviously never heard the old maxim that what is said below stairs stays below stairs. Thankfully the rest of the visit passed off uneventfully and the Hargrove WI ladies left, still chatting and smiling, enthusing about what a lovely time they had had.

Almost as soon as I had closed the front door as the last of the ladies left I heard my name being called from the drawing room.

'Rosie, can I have a word with you?' Lady Linton did not sound pleased.

'Yes, Lady Linton.' I braced myself and entered the room.

'I would rather you did not discuss matters relating to the daily routines of this house with perfect strangers.' Her eyes fairly blazed at me.

'Sorry, Lady Linton.' I mumbled.

'If you have an issue with your duties here at Threldale Hall then I would prefer you to discuss it with me first,' she continued.

'Yes, Lady Linton.'

'Do you have anything you wish to talk to me about?'

'No, Lady Linton.'

'Well, in future you will keep matters concerning Threldale Hall and what goes on inside its walls confidential. Do I make myself clear? For now we shall consider the matter closed. You may continue with your duties.'

'Yes, Lady Linton.' My ears were positively burning.

On the whole I think I got off lightly. In future I would be a lot more careful about what I said to people visiting Threldale. As for Mrs Waltroyd, she would be given a wide berth should I happen to see her either in the village or walking on the estate. I couldn't see me joining the Hargrove WI any time soon either.

The School Outing

It was a bright sunny morning, a rare occurrence in a dale that seemed to attract rain, when Lady Linton received a call from Hargrove Primary School. The teacher of the first year pupils was looking to make a history project they were doing about old houses and old families more interesting for her class of five-year-olds by arranging a visit to Threldale Hall. Lord and Lady Linton did not usually encourage these kinds of visits to Threldale, especially after their rather uncomfortable experience with the president of the Hargrove WI.

Hargrove Primary School, with a roll of fewer than a hundred children in total, wasn't a very big school, but it did take children from a few outlying small communities in the area in addition to those from the local farms and Hargrove village itself. Being born and raised in the dale and having parents who were forthright in their opinions meant the children were a tough bunch, who were used to hard winters and rugged landscapes. It also meant that for those families who had lived in the dale for generations, had an inborn sense of loyalty towards both the village of Hargrove and Threldale Hall as well as the dale it sat in, and they looked to Lord and Lady Linton to show their commitment to the village.

Things had been quiet for the last few weeks at Threldale and Lady Linton was in a particularly good mood, so she agreed that the teacher and her class of five-year-olds would be more than welcome to come and have a look around Threldale. There was some discussion regarding a mutual date and time, and an appointment was made to suit both the school timetable and Lady Linton. I didn't get involved until I took the tea tray into the drawing room at 11 30 a.m., and that was when Lady Linton raised the subject of the school visit with me.

'Rosie, we are to have some small visitors to Threldale. Hargrove Primary School are studying country houses as part of a history project they are working on. I have agreed that they can come here and we will give them a bit of a talk about the old days, when we needed an entourage to run the place. We can show them some of the more interesting rooms below stairs, as it were. I don't think we need to include the main reception rooms with the antiques or paintings this time, as that would be a subject of little interest to five-year-olds. We will need to find something else that will be of interest to them.'

'Yes, Lady Linton.' I knew exactly what was about to come my way, and it didn't involve 'we' in any way.

'All in all you did a good job with the Hargrove WI, if we disregard the indiscretions of certain conversations you had with their president. That woman was quite insufferable. Anyway, I have absolute confidence that

I can leave this particular visit in your hands. The teacher of this class is an altogether different kettle of fish to the awful Mrs Waltroyd.' The WI visit had not gone well from my point of view, partly because it had ended with Lady Linton having some sharp words with me.

'Yes, Lady Linton.'

I assumed that this group would be easier. It was young children and not adults. The teacher's attention would be on the children at all times, and not on what I did as housekeeper of Threldale. I remembered with embarrassment that, as part of the preparations for the Hargrove WI visit, I had discussed my work as housekeeper with Mrs Waltroyd who had then conversationally told Lady Linton what I had said. It was my own fault. I should have been a lot more guarded about what I talked about. I foolishly thought she was aware of the unwritten rule that what is said below stairs stays below stairs. I would not make the same mistake again.

'The teacher is called Miss Peters and she will be bringing her class of five-year-olds here a week on Friday, and we will have to entertain them for about an hour. They will be walking up from the village school and should arrive here around 10 a.m. She has around fifteen children in her charge. I have no idea what would interest a five-year-old, but I am sure you will think of something,' she continued.

'Yes, Lady Linton.' So again I was to play host to a group of visitors to Threldale. This was getting to be a habit, and an unwelcome addition to my already heavy workload. I could only hope that Miss Peters would be easier to work with than Mrs Waltroyd had been. As I would not be meeting Miss Peters before the visit I would have to work out the details on my own.

So, despite my gaffe with Mrs Waltroyd, Lady Linton was going to trust me with this tour for the class of five-year-olds. The more I thought about it the more I knew I had no more idea of what would interest a child of that age than Lady Linton did. Time to put my thinking cap on. I had just over a week to come up with something interesting, engaging and interactive.

I spent any spare time I had over the next few days wandering in and out of various rooms, and in particular looking through all the boxes stored in the old servants' bedrooms in the attic. In the process I got very dirty (I made a mental note to thoroughly clean these unused rooms next time I had a spare few hours). These bedrooms had last been used when Threldale had a full complement of servants, which had been more than seventy-five years ago. So, they were a bit musty, dusty and full of cobwebs, and were now only used to store unwanted furniture.

Slowly, over time, bits and pieces of the talk I was planning started to fall into place. I would concentrate on the life of the servants below stairs rather than the family above stairs. That might interest the children more. In order to keep their interest during the visit I would have to make it a hands-on experience as much as I could. I would have to clean up the attic enough to take a group of children up there without them falling over piles of junk or getting dirty. I would need to decide which rooms off the Kitchen passage could be made to appear exciting to a five-year-old.

In a box in one of the old servants' bedrooms I found some old cream-coloured chamber pots that I thought would amuse the children. From what I remembered of my own childhood, all children love a bit of toilet humour. The pots just needed a bit of a wash to get rid of the years of accumulated grime. I also found some rather pretty bowl and jug sets. They had lovely bunches of roses painted on them, but they too would need a wash before I could use them.

I cleared one of the servants' bedrooms of junk and, after brushing off all the dust and cobwebs, set it up with an old cast-iron bed frame and a horsehair mattress. Next I made the bed up with sheets, blankets and an old pillow, as if it was to be slept in by some poor servant. I found an old rickety wardrobe and a battered pine dresser, both of which I managed to manhandle into the room after much puffing and panting. I pushed a washed chamber pot under the bed, just as it would have been a century ago. The final touch was to put the (now clean) rose-painted bowl and jug on the pine dresser. The room now looked ready for occupation by one of the housemaids.

I went through an old household accounts book from a hundred years ago that had been kept by one of the old butlers, and was able to find out how many servants it took to run Threldale back then. I made a note of the job titles of those servants and how many there were. Finally I found some candles, some old candlesticks and some slightly rusty oil lamps to clean up and use. I even found a box containing some old pottery hot-water bottles with their cork bungs still in place. I would fill one of these up on the day and put it in the bed I had made up, after I had made sure it wasn't going to leak.

I now had a rough outline of what I was going to tell the children and, probably more importantly, what I was going to show them. I ran my plan past Lady Linton just to make sure she was happy with it. She seemed happy that the children would spend most of the time in the unused parts of the house and she would not have to interact in anyway with them during their visit.

The Friday morning of the school visit arrived, and I had been up since 5 30 a.m. in order to clear as many of my chores as possible before the school party were due to arrive at 10 a.m. Lady Linton would expect no less from me. Just before they were due to arrive I filled the hot-water bottle, checked for leaks, and nipped up to the attic bedroom to put it in the bed. I was going to get one of the children to check if the bed was warm as part of the below-stairs experience.

Right on time the front doorbell chimed, and Lady Linton welcomed Miss Peters and her class of five-year-olds to Threldale Hall. She introduced me as the housekeeper and handed everything over to me, stating that I knew as much as her, if not more,

41

about how the hall was run a century ago and that I would be taking them round. With that she promptly disappeared into the drawing room, pleading pressing correspondence. I have never known someone have so much pressing correspondence.

'Hello, Miss Peters. Hello, boys and girls. As Lady Linton said, I am the housekeeper here at Threldale, and everyone who knows me calls me Rosie.' I began, 'Today I am going to show you how a house like this was lived in – and run by the servants – a hundred years ago, rather than how the Linton family lived. I hope you all enjoy your visit.'

There were lots of eager faces looking up at me, waiting to see what I would say or do next. Miss Peters asked if she could take photographs on the way round that the children could use back at school to write up the project. I couldn't see a problem with that but, bearing in mind the roasting I got for crossing boundaries regarding confidentiality with Mrs Waltroyd, I asked that a copy of the pictures be made available for Lady Linton to approve beforehand, to which Miss Peters readily agreed.

I set off up the main staircase with the class following me and Miss Peters bringing up the rear. We then took the narrow service stairs up to the old servants' bedrooms on the attic floor and went into the room I had previously set up. I went through a typical day for a housemaid, from rising at five to going to bed as late as midnight, tired from a long day of endless chores. I went through some of the chores she may have done, from cleaning out fires, sweeping carpets, scrubbing floors and polishing furniture, through washing laundry, pressing clothes and mending, to serving, clearing and cleaning up after meals.

There were lots of 'ooh!'s from the children and plenty of questions about when the housemaid could stop for a break, what meals she got, when she stopped for them, whether or not she was paid or got any holidays, and if she could go home to her family at the end of the day. Miss Peters made sure they put their hands up so that I could answer their questions one at a time.

I knew the answer to some of these questions but I had to just do the best I could with the limited knowledge I had for quite a few. They were surprised at the amount of work the housemaid had to do in a day and just how little time she had off. I would like to have added that the amount of work to do in a day had not changed in a hundred years – only the number of staff doing it had – but I refrained for reasons of self-preservation.

Now I was going to have some fun. I reached under the bed and pulled out the chamber pot.

'What do you think this was used for?' I asked.

There were a lot of blank faces.

'Well, a hundred years ago there were no toilets or bathrooms in houses like this. There was no hot and cold running water, no baths, no showers, no toilets and no handbasins. This is a chamber pot, and it would have been used at night if you needed to go to the toilet. Every bedroom had a chamber pot. It didn't matter whether you were family or one of the

43

servants.'

Now the faces now showed disbelief.

'No toilets, Miss?' piped up a voice from the back of group.

'No toilets. Now, it was the job of the housemaids to go round all the bedrooms to empty and clean the chamber pots as part of their morning duties. Not a very nice job, and probably a bit smelly too.' I was getting into my stride.

The look of disbelief had changed to horror.

'That's disgusting, Miss!' came the voice from the back again.

I put the chamber pot back under the bed. Now it was time to get one of the children to check under the bedclothes.

'Who would like to put their hand down between the sheets to see what it feels like to sleep under blankets?' I asked.

Lots of hands shot up, and I pointed at a little girl in pigtails with a sparkly top and red leggings.

'Would you like to come here beside the bed and just push your hand here? Don't worry. I'll show you where.'

I encouraged her to come forward, and she wriggled her way through her classmates until she was by the bed. She looked at me for direction, so I lifted the covers slightly and she put her hand underneath.

'Ooh! It's warm, Miss!' she giggled.

She pushed her hand further underneath.

'I can feel something, Miss.' She was quite excited at her discovery.

'It's an old-fashioned hot-water bottle,' I explained.

I pulled the covers right back to reveal the hot-water bottle, and there were squeals of delight as they took it in turns to touch the bottle, which was still warm.

'Why don't they have soft and fluffy hot-water bottles like mine, Miss?' asked a boy at the front of the group, who was dressed in a Leeds United outfit.

'There was no rubber or plastic to make a soft water bottle, and it certainly would not have been covered in anything to make it a bit softer. It had to be made out of something hard that would hold hot water. You had to be very careful when it was full because it would break if you dropped it,' I continued.

Next I moved them over to the pine dresser, where I showed them the pretty rose-painted bowl and jug set.

'Each morning the housemaids would have brought hot water in a jug just like this one and it would have been poured into a bowl like this one, and this would be used to have a wash. This would not have been used by any of the servants, though. Only the family and any guests staying here would have used these bowls and jugs. This was instead of having a bath or a shower. Servants would have to wash using the cold tap in the scullery off the Kitchen. I will show you later, when we go downstairs, where the servants would have been able to have a wash.'

I then took them back down the service stairs and the main staircase then through the passage door to the Kitchen, where I had set up the old candlesticks with candles and the oil lamps (which were now

45

cleaned up) on the scrubbed table.

'A hundred years ago there was no electricity, so when it was dark candles and oil lamps were lit all over the house. The servants would have to go round the rooms with a lighted taper and light the candles and oil lamps. I'll show you what I mean.'

I lit the candles and the oil lamps and then went around the Kitchen, closing all the wooden shutters. After stern warnings from Miss Peters to the children to stay away from the naked flames I went over to the light switch and turned off the lights. The room was now only dimly lit by the yellow glow from the candles and the oil lamps. I explained that this was once the only kind of lighting available once it got dark. I switched the lights back on and snuffed out the candles and oil lamps.

The light from the candles and oil lamps had caused lots of nervous giggling, as the children couldn't believe there was once no such thing as a light that could not be turned on and off instantly at a wall switch. They found it hard to believe that the only light in the rooms came from the naked flames of candles and lamps – especially as they had seen just how little light was given out compared to what they were used to.

Before leaving the Kitchen I took them to the scullery (I now used this room as the pantry), which was a smaller room off to the side of where the old cooking range used to be and where my Aga was now. This room felt colder than the Kitchen as it had a tiled floor and walls, which could be scrubbed to keep it clean. There were no windows in this room, and the only thing in there was an old enamel sink with long wooden boards on either side. There was just one tap over the sink, but it was a cold tap.

'This was where the servants would have had a wash when they needed one. It would have been very cold and uncomfortable. Not nearly as nice as having a jug of hot water and a bowl in your bedroom.' There were a lot of open-mouthed looks from the children.

'OK. We will now move upstairs to see where the family lived.'

The rest of the time was spent showing Miss Peters and her class the other side of life at the hall. I showed them the Dining Room and explained about formal place settings, meals and being served at the table. I also took them to see the unused billiard room, where the gentlemen of the house would retire in the evening to play snooker, and the Entrance Hall, where the family and guests would come and go, before returning to the servants' domain in the Kitchen. I didn't take them into Lord Linton's inner sanctum, the Library, because that would have been a room too far. He would not have liked a lot of children leaving sticky fingerprints anywhere in there. I didn't take them into the drawing room either, as that was where Lady Linton was working on her pressing correspondence.

Once we were all back in the Kitchen I gathered the children around the Kitchen table, having first removed the candlesticks and oil lamps to a safe place, and spent the last ten minutes covering the duties of the various other servants, such as the butler, the footman, the cook and the scullery maid. As a last item I brought out the list I had drawn up of the number of staff it had taken to run Threldale over a century ago.

'So back in 1910 Threldale Hall had a butler, a housekeeper, two footmen, two housemaids, a lady's maid, a valet, a cook and a scullery maid. Who can tell me how many servants that is altogether?'

Lots of hands shot up and I picked one at random.

'Please, Miss, it was ten, Miss.'

'That's right. Ten servants to run this house. Sometimes it was even more if there were a lot of guests staying.' I carried on. 'How many members of the Linton family do you think a staff of ten people looked after?'

There were lots of answers shouted out.

'Ten, Miss.'

'More than that, Miss.'

'He's being silly, isn't he, Miss?'

Miss Peters put her hand up and they all went quiet so I continued.

'Well, back in 1910 it was for just four: the Earl of Linton, who was Lord Linton's great-grandfather, his wife the countess and their two children, Edmund and Clarissa. Are you surprised that four people needed ten servants?'

Lots of nodding.

'That completes everything for today. Does anyone have any questions?' I finished.

There was a lot of shaking of heads but no questions.

'Have you enjoyed looking around Threldale?' I asked.

More nodding.

'What did you like best?'

Lots of little voices shouted at once, and while it was hard to hear any individual child I could clearly pick out four words repeated by quite a few of them, and those four words were,

'The Chamber Pot, Miss!' I should have known it would be something like that.

Finally, everyone trooped out of the Kitchen and back into the Entrance Hall ready to return to school. At this point Lady Linton reappeared from the drawing room to say goodbye. Miss Peters got all the children to say, 'Thank you Lady Linton,' in unison, and she gently pushed one of the boys forward towards Lady Linton. He shyly walked up to her and held out a thank-you card that had been made by the class in school the day before. Lady Linton took the card, smiled and said,

'Thank you, children.' The boy turned round and walked back to join his classmates.

Miss Peters thanked Lady Linton, said her goodbyes and led the crocodile line of children out of the front door to walk back through the estate grounds to their school in Hargrove. I closed the front door as the last child left and turned to go back to the Kitchen and put away the various items I had left out.

'Rosie, before you go... Do you think they enjoyed

the visit?' asked Lady Linton.

'Yes, Lady Linton. They seemed to enjoy themselves.'

'Do you think the school will want to send any other classes?'

'I don't know, Lady Linton.' I think Lady Linton feared she had opened a floodgate of visiting children. We would have to wait and see if that was the case.

The Restoration Project

£ord Linton was planning something big and I had no idea what it was, but it smelt like trouble for me. Over the previous few weeks there had been a succession of men in suits disappearing into the Library with him. Lady Linton knew a little about it, and from the look on her face she wasn't happy. I had overheard her quizzing him about what was going on and not getting any meaningful response.

Despite her many appeals for more information about what was going on, it was a few weeks before Lord Linton was finally prepared to discuss his plans in detail with her. He asked her to join him in the Library, where he could show her what he had been planning. It was then that he announced that those plans were now complete and there was to be extensive restoration work carried out on the unloved billiard room.

Threldale Hall was a large house and, of the reception rooms on the ground floor, only three were used on a regular basis: the drawing room, the Dining Room and the Library. Of course there was also the spacious Entrance Hall. All these rooms were well cared for by being dusted, polished and vacuumed by me routinely. They were also kept in good repair and in clean decorative order. The other rooms on the ground floor were not so lucky. The billiard room, the Orangery and the Morning Room were all closed up, unused and unloved.

Let me describe the state of the neglected billiard room that was to be restored. The walls were panelled from top to bottom in oak, and these panels would have been a wonderful sight when the room was in use a century ago as a gentleman's retreat from the ladies during the evening. But now some of the panels were missing and had been 'temporarily' replaced with odd bits of rough timber. Some of them were split or warped, and all of them were suffering from years of exposure to the sun and a general lack of care.

The large windows that bathed the room in sunlight during the day had more than a few cracked panes of glass in them but, luckily, none of them were actually missing. The paintwork on wood frames was flaky and discoloured and the wood was rotten in some places, leaving panes of glass in danger of falling out. Spiders, alive and dead, occupied every corner of the windows and filled those same corners with layer upon layer of dust-encrusted webs.

The carpet that ran around the snooker table in the centre of the room was faded. It was threadbare in some places and completely worn through in other places. The green baize on the snooker table was sun-bleached and ripped, revealing the slate panels beneath. The snooker balls were so sun-bleached it was difficult to distinguish between the different colours. The cues were so warped and bent they could only be used to pot balls around corners.

Over the years this room had been used as a dumping ground for anything and everything. As a result it was difficult to move around the room without bumping into or falling over boxes and old bits of furniture. It was a very sorry-looking room indeed, which was such a shame as it would have been a wonderful room in its heyday a century ago. If walls could talk then there would be some tales to tell about what went on in this room.

While Lord Linton was excited at the prospect of getting the billiard room restored and fit to be used again, Lady Linton was not so sure about the mess that would be generated to achieve this (she liked Threldale to be kept clean and tidy at all times). She had a long list of instructions for me before the work had even begun.

'Rosie, you are to make sure the dust and mess stay in the billiard room.' This was a difficult request where dust was concerned. It has a habit of drifting wherever it wants to. The Entrance Hall was going to get in a mess, purely because that was the best way for the builders to get to the billiard room from the front door. They could have used use the side door, but that would mean them carrying whatever they needed through the long and narrow Kitchen passage to reach the passage door, which would have to be propped open, and from there into the Entrance Hall.

'Rosie, you need to empty the billiard room of all

the boxes, furniture and other junk before the work starts.' I needed to find somewhere to put it all first, because there was an awful lot of junk to move out. Some of the boxes had been stored in there for so long that they were falling apart, with the contents spilling out across the floor. It was like navigating an obstacle course.

'Rosie, make sure any men in hobnail boots only have access to the Entrance Hall and the billiard room. I do not want you to let them wander anywhere else, and I certainly don't want to find any strange men upstairs.' That would be difficult, and would require me to watch them the entire time they were working in the house. I had my own chores to get on with without supervising the workmen while they went about the restoration.

'Rosie, make sure nothing gets broken during the work.' I had no idea how to stop breakages. The best thing I could do was to make sure there was nothing breakable within the areas where the builders were likely to operate. If there was nothing to to knock off any surface then there would be nothing to break.

'Rosie, the builders are not to leave any of their rubbish lying around when they go home.' My best bet with this one was to pick up the litter at the end of each day and to gather up anything lying around in the Entrance Hall and put it in the billiard room. I would need to tell the men that this was what I was going to do so that they would know not to leave anything lying around in the Entrance Hall that they didn't want me to touch.

'Rosie, I do not want to hear a lot of noise early in the morning once the work starts.' What should I do with this request? Get them to wear slippers and use velvet hammers? All I could do was keep shushing them in the morning until Lady Linton came down. They were going to love me. I could see me getting an uncomplimentary nickname before the work was done.

One Friday afternoon I was dusting and generally cleaning in the drawing room when Lord Linton came in looking for Lady Linton. He walked straight past me. I don't think he even saw me. She was sitting in front of the fire reading the paper when he just launched into a speech.

'Ah, there you are, dear. I have confirmed a start date with the building chappies. They are coming on Monday to start at 8 a.m. Shouldn't take too long, and once it is all finished we shall have to have friends round to give it a bit of a christening. If it all goes well we should look at restoring the Orangery and the Morning Room sometime in the future. Must pass on the old place on in better condition than we received it. Don't you agree?'

He didn't wait for an answer from Lady Linton. He just turned around, walked past me and out of the drawing room across the Entrance Hall and went into the Library, closing the door behind him. For Lord Linton that was quite a long speech.

Back in the drawing room, Lady Linton just looked at the door and then at me.

'The place is going to be a disaster area. You will have to work hard over the next few weeks to keep Threldale clean and tidy, Rosie.'

'Yes, Lady Linton.' Didn't I always work hard?

'We will still be receiving visitors while the work is going on, and I do not want them walking into a building site,'

'Yes, Lady Linton.' I wanted to point out that it was going to be a building site no matter what I did to keep on top of it.

'You will need to get the billiard room emptied straight away. Once you have done that let me know and I will inform Lord Linton the room is ready for Monday morning.' I had a bad feeling that Lady Linton was going to be a little short-tempered over the coming weeks and I would be well advised to stay out of her way as much as possible.

I set to, moving boxes, stuffed creatures, books and old bits of furniture out of the billiard room and into the old butler's room off the Kitchen passage, one of the few unused and empty rooms that had not been filled with junk. It was a very dusty and dirty job but, after a few hours of hard work, the billiard room was empty. The old butler's room was full of boxes and old furniture, but we were ready for the builders to arrive on Monday morning. I also covered everything in the Entrance Hall with dust sheets and, after having packed away everything small or breakable, I informed Lady Linton that the billiard room was ready for Monday morning. She in turn let Lord Linton know.

At eight o'clock sharp on Monday morning at least half a dozen burly men in dusty jeans, grubby T-shirts, hard hats and steel toe-capped boots arrived and trooped through the hall and into the billiard room, where Lord Linton was waiting for them. He was in his element directing operations, giving instructions, changing his mind, changing it back again and generally getting in the way. Lady Linton was conspicuous by her absence. I think she had taken refuge in the drawing room with the door firmly closed.

Over the next few weeks the builders would arrive at eight each morning and start work. I must have been the bane of their lives, telling them to watch out they didn't knock anything, to pick up rubbish, to remove tools and suchlike from the Entrance Hall and to keep the noise down. Regardless of me hounding them they were polite and hard-working, but I am sure that behind my back there was a lot of swearing and face-pulling aimed in my direction.

The windows were reglazed, the rotten woodwork was replaced, and all the woodwork was sanded and repainted. The floor was sanded and repolished and a new carpet was laid around the snooker table. The oak panelling was removed, repaired and refitted. Its missing pieces were replaced and then the whole lot was oiled several times, the colour darkening with each oiling and the wood becoming alive again.

The old baize was removed from the snooker table to reveal that two of the slate boards were broken.

New ones were ordered, delivered and fitted. New green baize covered the table, restoring it to its former glory. Modern suspended lighting was installed over the table. The final touch was a complete set of new snooker balls, cues and rests. The old ones were retired to the butler's room along with all the other junk.

During all this time I had to contend with Lady Linton becoming more and more frustrated with the dust, the mess, the noise and the disruption to her normal routine. She was not one to suffer such indignities in silence.

'Rosie, have you dusted and cleaned this morning?' I dusted every morning, afternoon and evening.

'Rosie, who walked this grit into the drawing room?' We all did, on the soles of our footwear.

'Rosie, who is that man going into the Library?' That was one of the many burly builders toing and froing.

'Rosie, why are there dirty mugs outside the front door?' I tried to keep on top of these by washing them and returning them to the builders.

'Rosie, what is that awful noise?' It could be a hammer, a drill, a sander or just the radio on too loud.

'Rosie, who left those half-eaten sandwiches on the hall table?' Not me!

I was not sure who was going to go mad first, Lady Linton or me.

It was with great relief when Lord Linton informed Lady Linton that all the work was complete and that, having inspected the completed work, he was thoroughly satisfied with the outcome and she was to come and take a look. The same could not be said of the building site that was the rest of the ground floor and the area outside the front door, now that the builders had left for the last time.

Lady Linton walked carefully through the mess that was the Entrance Hall to the door of the newly restored billiard room.

'Come in and take a look at the finished article, dear.' Lord Linton was keen to show off his new baby.

'Well, I must say it looks a lot better than I expected. They have made a good job of it. It is all very dusty in here, though, and the windows are quite dirty,' Lady Linton said as she entered the billiard room and walked slowly round the snooker table, stroking the baize and studying the restored oak panelling.

Out of nosiness, I followed her into the room.

'Rosie, I was just about to call you.' She had seen me coming in behind her. I wondered what she wanted, as if I couldn't guess.

'Yes, Lady Linton.'

'Now all the work has been completed in here you need to get the house cleaned up. You can start in here and move on to the Entrance Hall. The other rooms are dusty too. And don't forget outside the front door.'

'Yes, Lady Linton.' That would keep me busy over the next few days.

I left the two of them in the billiard room, closing the door behind me as I went. I could hear their muffled voices through the closed door, and I think

Lord Linton was having a hard time trying to convince Lady Linton that the finished result was worth all the noise, dust and disruption she had endured over the previous weeks. He would have to win her round if he wanted to restore either the Orangery or the Morning Room at Threldale.

The next morning, once the team of builders had paid a final visit to remove the last of their tools, materials and rubbish, I set to with dusters, mops, brushes and a vacuum. The dust sheets were shaken free of dust and grit outside then folded up and put in the laundry. They would need washing before I put them away. The furniture throughout the whole of the ground floor was washed down, as were all the floors. Once it was all dry I began the long job of polishing the furniture and waxing the floors.

It took two weeks of hard work in between my usual duties to get Threldale back to some sort of normality. Lady Linton spent that time checking the rooms as I finished each one, making sure it was up to her high standards by running her finger along ledges, peeking behind curtains and looking under furniture. To be honest I thought my own standards were pretty high and I did not expect her to be able to find fault, which she didn't.

Lady Linton approached me as I was gathering up all my equipment on finally completing the last of the clean-up operation.

'Rosie, Threldale looks like her old self. In future when we have any restoration work done you will have to try harder to keep on top of the mess.' The cheek! As if I hadn't been trying to do just that over the previous weeks.

'Yes, Lady Linton.'

'Now we are in a position for Lord Linton to invite friends round to see the restored billiard room.' She didn't sound like she was ready to invite friends. I think she would have preferred a few weeks to get over the stress.

It was decided that rather than have a formal dinner for invited guests they would have an unveiling party, where a few games of snooker could be played and refreshments provided in the form of drinks and some light bites. I groaned inwardly when Lady Linton informed me of the plan. It would mean lots of preparation beforehand and a late night of carrying round trays of either food or drinks, which would mean my feet would be aching by the end of the night.

Lady Linton summoned me from my sanctuary in the Kitchen to discuss her plans for the unveiling party.

'Rosie, we are going to invite around twenty people to the party but you won't have to cook for them, so it shouldn't be too onerous an evening for you.' I would be the judge of that.

'I am going to get caterers to provide a hot buffet served by waitresses,' she continued. 'I just need you to help them as necessary, as they will be using the Kitchen. Make sure they don't take away anything that belongs to Threldale.'

'Yes, Lady Linton,' I had a few questions but nothing that Lady Linton needed to answer.

Who were the caterers?

Had we used them before?

How many people would there be invading my domain?

What 'help' would I be providing?

What did Lady Linton think the caterers would take away that didn't belong to them?

I decided the best course of action was to wait until the evening of the party and just play it by ear.

The evening of the unveiling party arrived, as did the caterers. There was one chef, one assistant and two waitresses. They all introduced themselves to me with a smile and a handshake. It still felt strange, having people in my domain that I had no control over. Once the evening began I thought I would get away with just watching from the wings, but that wasn't to be.

'Do you have a bottle opener? Someone forgot to pack ours.'

'We were told you would provide napkins.'

'Where is the kettle?'

'Do you have any mugs we can use for tea for the workers?'

'We haven't brought enough trays. Can we borrow a couple?'

'I don't suppose you could help with the washing-up?

'Where is the loo?'

'Do you have any mayo?'

My evening turned out to be quite a busy one. I had no idea how the unveiling party went, as I never made it out of the Kitchen. I assume it all went all right, as the waitresses took full trays of hot food or cold drinks out to the guests and brought empty trays back. I kept on top of the washing-up of the constant stream of dirty dishes.

By the end of the evening all the food was gone, the dishes and glasses all washed and packed away in the caterers' boxes and the Kitchen looked as it did before they arrived. To my knowledge nothing had been packed that belonged to Threldale, and at eleven forty-five the caterers left with a cheery wave, thanking me for the cups of tea and all my help throughout the evening. It all sounded very quiet on the other side of the Kitchen passage door, so I went back into the Kitchen and sat down at the table for ten minutes with a well-earned cup of tea and a plate of nibbles that the caterers had very kindly kept back for me.

At midnight I slipped out of the Kitchen and peeped into the Entrance Hall to see what was going on. There was no one about. It would seem that all the guests had left. All the lights were still on but there was no sign of Lord or Lady Linton. I had to assume they had retired after the last guest had gone. I wandered around the various rooms looking for dirty plates and glasses but there were none. There didn't even seem to be any rubbish lying around. In fact everywhere was relatively tidy. That made a nice change.

I secured the doors, turned out the lights and retired

to my bed in my little flat at the top of the house, tired but relatively content. I hadn't had to cook the food, plate it up or serve it to the guests. I hadn't even seen the guests.

'I wish Lord and Lady Linton did more entertaining like this evening,' I said to myself.

The Film Crew

'Rosie! Rosie! Where are you?' Lady Linton was standing in the middle of the Entrance Hall, waiting for me to miraculously appear from wherever I happened to be working.

'Here, Lady Linton.' I came out of the Dining Room where I had just finished polishing the table, so I was a little pink from my exertions.

'Ah, there you are. Have you heard of a television programme called *Dalehead View*?'

'Yes, Lady Linton. I believe it is a soap opera set in a fictional Yorkshire town, although I have never watched it.' *I never have time to watch anything*, I added inside my head.

'Well, I had never heard of it until today. I have just been talking to a young man on the telephone about the programme. Apparently the programme-makers need a location that they can use for a storyline set in a country hotel. With that in mind they are coming to look at Threldale Hall as a possibility. There is nothing definite yet. I need you to find out more about this – what did you call it? Soap? – before anything is agreed. You will know how to find out that kind of information, besides which I just don't have the time.'

'Yes, Lady Linton.' A job for the evening when I was supposed to be off duty with my feet up in my little flat at the top of Threldale.

Threldale Hall looked out across large lawns surrounded by shrubbery and woodland, and on towards open farmland and the rugged slopes of the hills that climbed up either side of our lovely dale to the bracken and heather-crowned tops. It would be a good location for a country hotel, if a little isolated, and I could see why the makers of *Dalehead View* were looking at it as a location. On a clear, sunny day there was no place better to be. It would also bring in some welcome business to the local shop and the pub in Hargrove.

That evening, when I retired to my flat, I did some research on the programme, the background, the characters and some of the storylines. Should Lady Linton ask me for more information about it I was now in a position to pass on my knowledge. From what I was able to learn about it I can't say that it was a programme that appealed to me. It seemed to lurch from scandal to disaster to misery with not a lot to cheer one up in between. Lord and Lady Linton had televisions in their respective dressing rooms and there was one in the drawing room but as far as I was aware they hardly ever switched them on except for the Queen's speech on Christmas Day and maybe the news, should there be an item in the newspaper that they wished to know more about. They had no interest in soaps, quiz shows, films or documentaries, preferring to read newspapers, magazines and books.

Over the next few weeks there were a lot of comings and goings by various groups of people connected with the Dalehead View production company, working out possible set layouts, scenes and character placements. They wandered in and out of different rooms, waving clipboards about, talking among themselves and taking notes. During this time I was able to inform Lady Linton of what the soap was about, which I summed up as the ups and downs, mainly downs, of everyday working people who lived on the same street in a fictional Yorkshire town. I don't think she was very impressed, but then I hadn't been impressed either.

Finally, the production company confirmed that Threldale Hall was to become the Grey Goose Hotel and Spa in an episode of *Dalehead View*. Two of the main characters were to be married at the location and, if my research was anything to go by, it would not go smoothly. A contract was drawn up and I heard a whisper that a rather large fee would be forthcoming to swell the coffers of Threldale Hall. I wondered whether Lady Linton would consider the disruption she was about to endure worth the figure being paid, but I doubted it. As for Lord Linton, he hated any upset to his routine at Threldale so he immediately arranged to stay with an old army chum in York for a couple of weeks while the filming was scheduled to take place.

Two days before the film crew and cast were due to arrive I was instructed by Lady Linton to prepare the Entrance Hall, the Dining Room, the drawing room and the main staircase ready for the arrival of the set designers the next day.

'Rosie, remove all ornaments, photographs and trinkets to somewhere safe where there is no chance of them being lost, misappropriated or broken. Make sure you remember where it all came from because everything will need to go back in exactly the same place.'

'Yes, Lady Linton.' I would need to label where everything came from so I could put it all back in the right place, as Lord and Lady Linton had a lot of trinkets covering the surface of every piece of furniture in the rooms that were going to be used for filming.

'And move as much of the furniture as you can out of harm's way too. I don't want anything to get scratched.'

'Yes, Lady Linton.'

'I expect all those who are coming here will treat Threldale with the respect it deserves, but we still need to be on guard in case of accidents.'

So for the rest of the day I removed, labelled and carefully stored everything I could carry into the newly restored billiard room for the duration of filming. By the time I was done it was packed full with barely an inch left to get anything else in, just as it had been before its restoration earlier in the year. The cleared rooms now looked bare and unwelcoming and, I am sorry to say, a little dusty in the harder-to-reach areas that were now exposed to view. I hoped Lady Linton would not spot the dusty corners before the rooms were filled with the 'Grey Goose Hotel' furniture. I am sure she would have something to say to me about not being thorough enough with my dusting.

The next day the set designers arrived and filled the newly emptied rooms with the hotel furniture. It looked cheap and tawdry. I could hear Lady Linton tutting as pieces were carried in with little care being taken to not bump into walls and doors, and chipping paintwork as they went. So much for the respect Lady Linton thought they would show Threldale. It was almost as if they thought of the house as just another set and not someone's home.

For my part I tried to stay out of the way as much as possible, down in the Kitchen. I would still be able to hear Lady Linton if she should summon me at any time. As for the set designers, they seemed to respect the contract agreement regarding which rooms could be used, if not the care of those rooms, and the wishes of Lady Linton to stay away from those parts of the hall deemed off limits. This was just the first wave of people. The film crew and actors had yet to arrive on site, and they might not be so respectful.

The day of filming arrived and so did a positive multitude of people. And they arrived very early, long before Lady Linton's normal rising time. Did television programmes really need this many people? When she appeared, over an hour after the first people had invaded Threldale, Lady Linton eyed them all with grave suspicion.

'Rosie, you must be on our guard. I didn't think there would be this many people,' she said in a stage whisper to me.

'Yes, Lady Linton,' I replied, also in a stage whisper.

'There is no way this number of people milling about will behave themselves. They will have no idea what has been agreed in the contract, and won't know to stay away from the private and personal parts of Threldale.'

'No, Lady Linton.'

'You must ensure that nobody strays into parts of the hall that they have no business to be in. I don't care who they or what their excuse may be.'

'Yes, Lady Linton.'

'That is down to you while they are here. I will be busy elsewhere, advising on set.'

'Yes, Lady Linton.' She was getting the hang of the lingo.

Now, quite how I was to police the access to the private parts of the house was beyond me. I had no idea who anyone was, there were so many of them. One thing I did know was that Lady Linton would not tolerate snoopers, and if she caught anyone not only would they be in trouble but I would be in trouble too. One thing I could do to head off any problems was to cordon off the main staircase somehow. I nipped into the billiard room where I remembered seeing a reel of red ribbon left over from Christmas. I used this to tie a barrier across the stairs. It wouldn't stop anyone, but hopefully it would deter them.

Filming began later that morning, with various members of the crew calling for, 'Quiet on set,' and 'Action!' I could see Lady Linton hovering about, watching to make sure nothing untoward went on that had not been agreed to. She was not going to brook any nonsense. The crowds of people filling the rooms might not know who she was, but if they stepped out of line in her eyes then they would soon find out.

In between trying to carry out my normal duties, in the rooms I still had access to, I would try my best to become invisible and patrol the parts of Threldale where no member of the cast or crew was permitted to stray. It wasn't long before Lady Linton's suspicions were proved correct. I caught a rather scruffy young man upstairs about to turn the handle of the door into Lady Linton's private suite of rooms. I actually watched him look over his shoulder first to check no one was watching him, but he didn't spot me standing at the top of the stairs. This wasn't a case of getting lost or looking for someone. This was blatant snooping.

'Excuse me,' I said. 'You aren't supposed to be up here.'

'Sorry, love, took a wrong turning,' he said. 'I was looking for the bathroom.'

'I am not your love. You must have crossed the red ribbon at the bottom of the stairs. That is not a wrong turn. I think you will find there are Portaloos provided outside in the grounds for the use of cast and crew.' Did he think I was stupid?

'All right, all right. Anyone can make a mistake.' He began walking towards me and the top of the stairs.

'No one is allowed upstairs for any reason. This part of the house is restricted and private.'

I didn't believe for one moment that he had taken a wrong turning. So much for the red ribbon deterring people. I ushered him back downstairs and pointed him at the outside facilities. He wasn't happy with me and I could hear him muttering something under his breath. Whatever it was I am sure it wasn't polite.

I would like to say that this was the only incident, but it wasn't. There were quite a few more over the next two days, caught by both Lady Linton and me in various private parts of the house. All had lame excuses.

'I thought we were filming in this room.' This was a man in his fifties, wearing a bright yellow bow tie, wandering around inside the Library and caught by Lady Linton while taking a book off a shelf.

'Does it not lead to an exit this way?' This was a woman with pink hair trying doorknobs in the Kitchen passage, caught by me.

'We were told by the owner that we could look around.' This was a couple of giggling make-up girls in shorts and T-shirts, caught by Lady Linton who, as the owner of the house, had sharp words with them.

'Don't you know who I am?' This was one of the so-called 'stars' of the show, who also claimed to know the Lintons personally and who, luckily, was caught by me. Another one who Lady Linton would have had sharp words with.

'This place is so big that I got lost.' I never managed to find out who this chap was. He was a bit cagey with his answers when I quizzed him (he was caught by me). I sincerely hoped he was with the film crew. We rarely had strangers wandering about on the estate, much less wandering into the house uninvited.

'I was told we could use the Kitchen to make ourselves a cuppa. Saves a walk out to the catering truck.' As if I would let just anyone use my Kitchen! They were caught by a rather irritated me and chased back into the Entrance Hall.

'It's all right. I'm a friend of the family.' Who do these people think they are kidding? Another one caught by me.

By the end of the second day, when filming had finished and people were starting to leave, I noticed that Lady Linton was showing signs of bad temper. Lots of them were wishing her a cheery good evening on their way out, but she was either scowling or snapping at them as they passed. Some of them looked quite shocked at her response to them.

On more than one occasion over the previous days she had spoken quite severely to the team headed up by the site coordinator, who was supposed to ensure the terms of the filming agreement were adhered to. Apparently the terms had been not so much broken as ripped up into little pieces and thrown out of the window. I have seen Lady Linton when she truly reaches the end of her patience, and it isn't a pretty sight. I was going to get it in the neck when they had all gone, so it was down to me to sort it out. There was no way I was taking any flak that wasn't mine.

First thing on the morning of the third and final day of filming, before Lady Linton came down, I decided that something needed to be done to rescue the relationship between her, the cast and the film crew so that she wouldn't take it out on me. I tracked down the one person who could sort it out: the site coordinator. Not an easy job with so many people milling about. This person was supposed to be the contact point between Lady Linton and the film crew. He should have been nipping her concerns in the bud instead of allowing them to fester as they had. I was sent on several wild goose chases by various members of the film crew before I found him surrounded by at least half a dozen people who seemed to consider themselves important.

'Right,' I muttered to myself. 'Here we go.'

'Excuse me, are you the site coordinator?' I said as loudly and as sternly as I could, putting on my best strict housekeeper face and pushing my way through the throng.

'Yes, and I'm busy! Go away!' This man was behaving appallingly. No wonder Lady Linton was getting so stressed out.

'Well, you had better spare me five minutes of your time right now or any goodwill you have here will be gone for good.' I glared at him with as much anger as

I could muster. I could be really stern when I put my mind to it, a trick I had learnt from Lady Linton on a bad day.

'And who are you?' he snapped at me.

'I am Lady Linton's housekeeper and you will listen to what I have to say,' I snapped back.

'All right. You have five minutes of my time and that's it.' He was an impatient man. However, having the employer that I did, it was something I was used to and I was not easily put off by it.

I should apologise for what followed but I wouldn't mean it if I did. I spent my allotted five minutes complaining loudly and expansively about the snooping and said how much it was upsetting Lady Linton ... how she felt her trust was being abused ... how she felt ignored. I laid it on as thick as I could. Lady Linton wasn't sleeping, with all the worry. She wasn't eating properly. It was proving to be an experience she wouldn't be repeating. The bad behaviour of some of the people on site was leaving a very bad taste in her mouth. He wasn't the one who would have to pick up the pieces after filming was finished. That would be me, as her housekeeper, and I did not see why I should be on the receiving end of a reprimand that should be aimed at him.

I paused, drew breath and carried on. This was not an environment Lady Linton was used to, and allowances should have been made. Everyone seemed to forget that this was her home and not some disposable film set they were invading. They might think they had paid to use Threldale as they pleased, but they had to remember using this house was a privilege not a right. As the site coordinator he needed to sort it out by whatever means he had at his disposal.

He looked at me with his mouth opening and closing like a fish. I don't think he had ever had an irate housekeeper ranting at him.

'I will leave it with you to sort it out, then?' I finished, and before he collected his wits I left him to carry on with whatever he was doing before my arrival.

As far as I am aware there were no snoopers on that last day of filming. I certainly didn't catch anyone. I did see the site coordinator talking to Lady Linton about mid morning and assumed my little outburst had done the trick. She did look a lot happier and seemed calmer when I served up lunch. Filming finally finished at 6.30 p.m., and then the set designers started to pack away the mountain of equipment that seemed to have taken over Threldale. The film crew and cast all got in their cars and left, so it was down to the set designers to dismantle and pack everything up. They finally left at 8.30 p.m., promising to return the following morning to finish packing up. As it turned out it was the evening of the next day before all the equipment was gone and the rooms were empty.

Early on the morning after that a white van pulled up outside the front door and the driver jumped out, went to the rear doors, opened them up and rummaged inside. He lifted out a large box and put it down on the gravel. He disappeared into the back of the van again and reappeared with the largest bouquet of flowers I have ever seen. It was huge.

'Hi there! I'm from *Dalehead View*. You know, the television programme? They were filming here up until a couple of days ago. I have a delivery for a Lady Linton that needs signing for.'

'I'll sign for it on her behalf. I'm the housekeeper here,' I said. This was a nice surprise.

'It is from all the cast and crew of the programme. Just a small thank-you to Lady Linton for her generous hospitality in making everyone feel so welcome.'

This was so unexpected, and I would like to think my little outburst had had something to do with it. I signed for the flowers and the box and had the driver put them on the table in the Entrance Hall to be dealt with by Lady Linton. I was curious to know what was in the box but I would have to wait until she came down to breakfast to find out.

I had plenty to do. Before putting everything back I vacuumed the empty rooms and dusted all the skirtings. Only then were all the ornaments, photographs, trinkets and furniture returned to their proper places. I was so glad that I had put labels on them all. That made the job so much easier. As I went along I made copious notes of any knocks, bangs and scrapes made to walls, doors and floors, of which there were quite a few. I got quite carried away and didn't hear Lady Linton come down, but I did hear the summons a minute or so later.

'Rosie! Rosie! Where are you?'

'Coming, Lady Linton.'

'When did the flowers arrive? What is in this box?

Who sent them? Did they leave a message?' One question at a time would have been nice.

'A van delivered them just after eight this morning. They are from the *Dalehead View* production company.'

'How lovely, and such a nice gesture!' she cooed. 'Find me something to open the box with. Quickly now!'

I went to the Kitchen, grabbed a pair of scissors and hurried back to Lady Linton. She used them to cut the seal around the box, lifted the flaps and then peered inside.

'Champagne! It's a dozen bottles of champagne!' I don't think I have ever seen Lady Linton so excited over a thank-you gift.

'And the flowers. Aren't they lovely? Such a beautiful big bouquet. Get them into water straight away. Find some nice vases for them. We will need three or four at least. Don't just stand there!'

'Yes, Lady Linton.' If that didn't put her in a good mood then nothing would.

Opera in the Garden

Just before lunchtime one cold but bright and sunny morning in spring, I was crossing the Entrance Hall from the door out of the Kitchen passage to the drawing room. I was on my way to collect a tea tray I had taken in earlier when guests had arrived to see Lady Linton. As I did so I could see Lady Linton saying goodbye to her guests at the front door and wondered who they had been. I had no doubt that if it was anything to involve me I would find out before the day was out, so I was not surprised when after lunch Lady Linton expressed a wish to talk to me in the drawing room. Hopefully I would find out who the guests had been, why they had been visiting Lady Linton and what my involvement was to be.

'Rosie, I have agreed to allow the Dales Operatic Society to hold a concert of famous opera arias on the front lawns of Threldale Hall. It will be quite a big event with a small orchestra, the singers and the audience. There will also be refreshments of some description laid on. None of it should affect us or the routine of the house.'

'Yes, Lady Linton.' I like a bit of opera but I hadn't heard or seen one in many years. This sounded like it was going to be interesting.

'It will need to be when we have the long summer evenings, so the date I have agreed with them is not for a couple of months. So there is nothing for anyone to do just yet.'

'Yes, Lady Linton.' I was already wondering what my duties and responsibilities were going to turn out to be on the day, though.

'We have initially arranged that it will begin at 7 p.m. on the Saturday evening. The concert is to raise funds for a local Dales charity so I am not charging for the use of the lawns. They have promised that after the concert they will return the lawns to state they found them in.'

'Yes, Lady Linton.' No fee for use of the lawns... That was a generous gesture by Lady Linton.

'I have agreed with them that they can have your services on the day for as long as they need them. I am sure it will only be for a couple of hours, and that can be your contribution to the charity.'

'Yes, Lady Linton.' Giving my time away for charity, as well. That was a surprise.

It would be a bit of a welcome change from my usual round of chores but I was a little wary regarding what I would be required to do, and whether or not it would still leave me time to carry out my normal duties. I hoped that on the day of the performance I would not be too busy and I would be able to listen to the music. In my younger days I went to quite a few operas and always enjoyed a good aria.

The organising committee of the operatic society

came two or three times over the next couple of months to agree with Lady Linton when the equipment could arrive, how many chairs would be set up for the audience, where a bar and buffet could be located, where the Portaloos could be discreetly placed and other mundane details. It was also agreed what time the committee could arrive to set it all up and the condition the lawns were to be left in once the concert was over.

My input to all this was zero. I did not even get to meet any members of the Dales Operatic Society. The services Lady Linton was promising I would provide would remain a mystery to me until the day of the performance, but it was only for a couple of hours so it shouldn't be too onerous. I was actually looking forward to helping out for a couple of hours in return for an evening of listening to opera arias.

As spring progressed into summer and the hours of daylight lengthened, the date of the event finally arrived bright and sunny. Most of it passed with no big changes to the usual routines at Threldale. I got all my chores completed and made, served and cleared away lunch.

It stayed quiet until about two in the afternoon, when the committee of the Dales Operatic Society, about five people, arrived to set everything up for the concert. Remembering Lady Linton's promise of my assistance, I let her know where I was going and went outside to join them on the lawns to see what they had planned for me. I would know, at last, what was they had in store for me.

'Are you the help Lady Linton promised?'

As I made my way across the lawns a middle-aged lady separated herself from the rest of the group and strode purposefully over to meet me.

'Yes. I'm Rosie, Lady Linton's housekeeper.'

I could feel myself grinning from ear to ear with anticipation.

'Right. Well, for the rest of today you are here to help me, understand? I will need your total commitment at all times.' The woman positively barked at me. My grin dropped from my face and I just nodded a bit nonplussed at being spoken to so sharply.

'My name is Mrs Barrington and I am chairperson of the Dales Operatic Society. Any questions this afternoon, consult me. No one else. I am the one with the master plan. There is a lot to do and we all need to pull together to get everything ready for this evening. I don't want you or anyone else, for that matter, disappearing off to do their own thing. I need to know where everyone is and what they are doing at all times. No exceptions. Do I make myself clear?'

'Yes, Mrs Barrington.' I felt as if I had just been given a good ticking off for being naughty. I was not so sure I was going to enjoy this experience after all. It was one thing Lady Linton being brusque with me but I was here to help as a favour to the society, not as some child sent to the headmaster's office for punishment.

Having made her point where I was concerned, she pointed at dozens of chairs stacked in piles on the driveway.

'You can begin by helping Agatha set out those chairs in rows on the lawns. Agatha is the lady in the straw hat and blue dress over there. She has been briefed by me on what to do. You may call her Miss Squires. Off you go, and when you have done that come back and see me. There will be plenty to keep you busy for the rest of the afternoon.'

What a bossy woman! I had a feeling that I was not going to be able to listen to any of the concert. I wasn't even sure I would get any kind of break.

I went over to see Miss Squires and find out how she wanted the chairs set out.

'Hello, Miss Squires. I'm Rosie, Lady Linton's housekeeper. Mrs Barrington has asked me to help you set out the chairs.'

'Thank you. Please call me Agatha. I hope Mrs Barrington wasn't rude to you. She can be a little overbearing when she is under pressure, but her heart's in the right place.' I wasn't sure that the indomitable Mrs Barrington had a heart, never mind in the right place.

'Shall we get these chairs sorted out into rows? Mrs Barrington has given me lots of detailed instructions about how she wants them to be put out for the audience over here and the small orchestra over there. They will be supporting the singers. Don't worry. I'll point you in the right direction as we go.'

'Thank you Agatha. I am all yours.' Agatha was much easier to like.

We spent the next hour carrying the chairs from the

driveway over to the lawns and setting them up in neat rows for the audience, and we also set up the chairs for the string quartet in their designated area. It was a warm afternoon so it was hard work putting out the chairs, and there seemed to be an awful lot of them. Agatha had her own supply of bottled water with her, which she generously shared with me. I wondered just how many people would be attending the performance.

Mrs Barrington came over a couple of times to see how we were getting on, to straighten out rows that we obviously hadn't put out straight enough for her high standards, and to make sure we were doing it according to the instructions she had given to Agatha. Once we had finished, Agatha and I went back to see what Mrs Barrington wanted doing next. I could have done with a quick five-minute break but that wasn't going to happen.

'You've finished the chairs, then, have you? Well, next the bar needs stocking with glasses. They are all in boxes over there. You will need to check they are clean, with no signs of water marks or lipstick residue. Hired glasses are never as clean as the suppliers would have you believe. If you find any marks you will have to wash and polish them. And then, once you are sure they are spotless, put them on the shelves in the bar area,' said Mrs Barrington as she pointed across the lawns to where the bar and buffet were being set up.

'Um, Mrs Barrington, do you have washing facilities for the glasses?' I asked warily.

'Do I look like I have washing facilities? Use your

84

initiative, for goodness' sake! Do I have to think of everything?' She boomed her answer at me, so I beat a hasty retreat to the bar area with Agatha.

Using my initiative, I told Agatha that I was fetching a bucket of warm water from the Kitchen in Threldale and some clean dry cotton tea towels and set off across the lawns. I didn't see Lady Linton, which was just as well, as I am not sure she would have approved of Threldale providing hot water and cloths for a function she wasn't even charging for. When I came back we began the job of cleaning and setting up the glasses for the bar. It seemed as if every glass we checked was dirty and needed washing, drying and polishing.

By the time 6 p.m. arrived the chairs were ready for the audience and the small orchestra, the bar was stocked with clean glasses and ready to serve refreshments and the buffet was ready to serve hot and cold snacks. I thought that was me finished for the day and I went to say my farewells to Agatha and the formidable Mrs Barrington. I was more than ready to return to my usual duties back inside Threldale and get supper organised for Lord and Lady Linton.

'Finished? We haven't finished. I need you here until the end of the performance. There are still lots of things that need doing. Lady Linton promised me your assistance for as long as I needed it. The whole point of this evening is to raise funds for a local charity. A few hours of your time is not a lot to ask, is it?' Mrs Barrington glared at me.

So much for just a couple of hours. It was up to four already. This woman did not seem at all pleased that I thought my services were no longer required. I wasn't at all pleased that she wanted my services until the end of the evening. On top of that, Lord and Lady Linton would not be at all pleased to find me missing for the whole of the evening. As I had expected to be back inside Threldale by the end of the afternoon I had done nothing about supper.

Mrs Barrington was still glaring at me as if I had said something unforgivable, and carried on listing jobs for me to do.

'The next job is to go around the whole area picking up all the rubbish left lying about after the set-up. Check where the cars were parked for unloading, then in between the rows of chairs. Don't forget the bar area and the buffet area. Take a couple of black bin bags with you. Our audience is due to start arriving within the next fifteen minutes, and I want everywhere to be clean and tidy.' I smiled at Mrs Barrington through gritted teeth and went off to make sure there was no rubbish lying about.

Once I had done this I took the opportunity to pop back into Threldale, hopefully without Mrs Barrington seeing me, to see if Lord and Lady Linton were all right with my being unavailable all evening. Lady Linton was not happy, though she had little choice but to let me carry on as she had promised my services for as long as they were required. She just didn't think they would be required for this long. I was able to point her at some leftovers in the Kitchen that would have to pass for a meagre supper, but I didn't have time to plate it up or set up the Dining Room before I had to go back outside.

I was missing for less than ten minutes, but when I got back outside the chairs were filling up with the audience and the bar and the buffet were doing a roaring trade providing refreshments. I looked around for Mrs Barrington. Unfortunately she found me before I found her. She came striding towards me as I walked back across the lawns.

'Where did you disappear to? While you are here to help I must insist that you do not wander off. Right now I need you to help guiding people to their seats, showing them where the bar area is and where to find the facilities.' She really was a fearsome woman. She made Lady Linton look like a pussycat.

The performance started on time at 7 p.m., and for the rest of the evening I was sent here and there to help out wherever necessary – checking the Portaloos, picking up rubbish, and gathering up dirty glasses, used napkins and paper plates. I would like to say I enjoyed the concert but I don't remember much about it because I was far too busy. So much for being able to listen to it. I didn't dare sit down or even stop moving in case I was spotted by Mrs Barrington.

By the end of the performance at nine thirty my feet ached and I was hungry, thirsty and grumpy. I had not sat down or had a rest of any sort since I had come out to help at 2 p.m. The audience, however, did enjoy the music, and many passed favourable comments on their way out to me and to the various members of the Dales Operatic Society. I was pleased that at least the audience had enjoyed the evening.

As dusk fell, the lawns finally emptied of people. Now it was just the Dales Operatic Society committee and me left as the stars came out. Mrs Barrington once again separated herself from the group to speak to me. I had been loitering about waiting to be dismissed. There was no way I was going to incur the wrath of Mrs Barrington by going back to Threldale without her express permission to do so.

'That's us finished for this evening. You may tell Lady Linton that we will be back first thing tomorrow morning to clear everything up. You go and put your feet up. You've worked hard today and earned a rest. I will make sure Lady Linton knows just what a great help you have been to us today. We will see you in the morning bright and early, when you can help out with the clearing up. Goodnight.' Mrs Barrington smiled graciously at me then turned to rejoin the members of the committee as they gathered together to leave.

With that final word to me she left, with the rest of the committee falling in behind her. I saw Agatha smile and wave at me as she left. I dragged myself back to Threldale and into the Kitchen. I kicked off my shoes, made myself a cup of tea and a quick sandwich to have while I sat by the Aga. Once I was done I switched off the lights, closed and locked the doors and retired upstairs to my flat, where I finally fell to my bed, exhausted, at 11 p.m. I had no idea how Lord and Lady Linton had coped without my services as they had already retired when I returned to the house. So while it was not a late night it was a very tiring and thankless one.

The next morning revealed a disaster area on the front lawns. As it was dark by the time everyone had gone the night before, I had not appreciated just how much of a mess had been left behind at the end of the performance. There were chairs everywhere. They were no longer in neat rows and not all were upright. There were dirty glasses on the bar, next to chairs or just abandoned on the lawns. As for rubbish, there were dirty paper plates, screwed-up napkins, plastic forks, half-eaten food and empty packets of snacks everywhere. Lady Linton was going to have a fit when she got up and looked out of her bedroom window.

As expected, when Lady Linton came down to breakfast she was not in a good mood.

'Rosie, have you seen the front lawns?' she exclaimed.

'Yes, Lady Linton.'

'How could they leave such a mess?' Somebody was going to get a roasting. I just hoped it wasn't going to be me.

'Sorry, Lady Linton. It was dark when they left.'

'They are coming back to clean it all up?'

'Yes, Lady Linton.'

'When?'

'This morning, Lady Linton.'

'And I don't suppose they said when this morning? I expected the lawns to be left as they found them. I want to see whoever is in charge as soon as they get here! If I had thought for one minute that you would be out there all afternoon and evening I would never have offered your services.' She was quite pink with indignation.

As it was nobody appeared at all during the morning, despite the promise given to me by Mrs Barrington. It was the middle of the afternoon before the committee members finally turned up to begin clearing the mess of the previous day, and once again they were headed by the formidable Mrs Barrington. From my vantage point in the Dining Room, where I was clearing away a late lunch, I could see her coming to the front door of Threldale Hall. Before she could even ring the doorbell a rather irate Lady Linton had opened the door and was glaring at Mrs Barrington. It was not difficult to hear what she said and I was going to enjoy listening to every word. Mrs Barrington was about to meet her match.

'You were supposed to be here this morning to clear up this mess!' blazed Lady Linton.

'Were we? Yes, I suppose we were. Got a bit caught up doing other things. Never mind. We are here now. Is Rosie ready to give us a hand with the clearing up?'

Mrs Barrington did not even seem to notice that Lady Linton was furious.

'Mrs Barrington, as well as free use of the lawns here at Threldale, I offered you the services of Rosie for the day of the concert. I also, rather foolishly, believed you would only need her for a couple of hours, not the eight hours you commandeered her for. I find that a blatant disregard of good manners. At no point yesterday did you consult me about whether or not I needed her here. So I am sorry, but she is busy with her other duties today. I cannot possibly spare her.'

Mrs Barrington looked gobsmacked, but Lady Linton hadn't finished.

'Last night you promised Rosie that you would be back first thing this morning to clear this mess up, and I would have expected someone of your standing in the community to keep their word. The fact that you finally turn up hours late means I have strong reservations about any future dealings we may have. Good day!'

Lady Linton then shut the door, leaving an astonished Mrs Barrington on the doorstep. There are times when I find Lady Linton exasperating, but not on this occasion. I was actually proud of the way she took down the pompous Mrs Barrington a peg or two.

It took the committee the rest of the afternoon and into the early evening to restore the front lawns to something nearing their former state. I could see Mrs Barrington directing the work, sending people here and there with chairs, bin bags and boxes. Everything was slowly but surely packed into the back of various vehicles.

Once or twice I caught sight of Agatha, looking a bit fraught. As for the lawns themselves, there was not a lot they could do about the wear and tear to the grass. But that would recover over the coming weeks under the tender ministrations of Sam and Don. The Portaloos would be picked up on Monday morning, so they were the only thing left by the time the committee, headed by Mrs Barrington, left Threldale.

At last peace was restored. I didn't hear Lady Linton mention the Dales Operatic Society after that evening, but I am almost certain it would be a very long time before their members would be allowed to perform in the grounds of Threldale again. As for the formidable Mrs Barrington, even if I never see her again I doubt I will forget her, much as I would like to.

The Goth Wedding

Summer was rolling on and things were getting busy at Threldale Hall. Master Ted, or should I say Edward Haydn Bertram Linton, eldest son of Lord and Lady Linton and heir to Threldale Hall, was home from Oxford for the summer. There was always more to do around the place when Master Ted was home. He was not the tidiest of people and tended to leave a trail of dirty clothes and dishes, magazines, newspapers and unwanted correspondence behind him wherever he went. There were extra rooms to clean, extra laundry to deal with and extra portions to cook at mealtimes.

This year, in addition to looking after Master Ted as well as Lord and Lady Linton, a couple of friends of Master Ted's were to be married in the grounds of Threldale Hall, and they would be staying for a few days before the ceremony. This would be a first. There had never been a wedding held in either the hall or the grounds.

According to the information Lady Linton had given to me the ceremony was to take place in the old tumbledown folly that sat on a small rise at the far end of the front lawns. This folly was supposed to add an air of romance to the view from Threldale, as if the views of the dale, the hills rising either side and the heather- and bracken-crowned tops weren't romantic enough.

The folly was supposed to represent the ancient ruins of a castle, and as such the walls were broken, crumbling and overgrown with brambles, nettles and other rampant weeds. It was also quite dark and gloomy. Apparently this is what had attracted the happy couple to Threldale. They were goths, and wanted the ceremony to take place somewhere suitably dark and gloomy.

Personally I found the folly quite creepy and avoided the place if I was out and about in the estate grounds, and certainly when it was dark or stormy. There were far too many shadows about the place for my liking. Sam and Don would have to do a lot of clearing of undergrowth and checking of the stability of the walls before the folly could be used for anything, never mind a wedding.

The wedding was to be followed by a reception in a marquee on the front lawns. Caterers would be on hand to prepare and serve the food. At least this part of the wedding would be more conventional. It would mean that I would have no involvement in the preparation or serving, much to my delight. The bride, Miss Suzi Chambers, her mother, Mrs Chambers, and the groom's mother, Lady Crichton-Banks, had organised menus, table settings, seating arrangements and flower displays. They had already had many discussions with a selected caterer, who would fulfil the menu requirements and provide all the staff.

The groom, the Honourable Alvin Crichton-Banks, only son of Lord and Lady Crichton-Banks, was due to arrive the week before the wedding and his bride, Miss Suzi Chambers, two days later. Alvin and Master Ted had been friends throughout their school years and had spent many summer holidays together, alternating between Threldale and Alvin's parents' home in Surrey. In later years they had learnt to ski during winter holidays in Austria. Now they were up at Oxford, both studying law and still close friends. This also meant that, as well as using Threldale as the location for the wedding and reception, Master Ted, as his oldest and closest friend, was to be Alvin's best man.

The Chinese bedroom was to be pressed into service for the happy couple to use on their wedding night. This room housed a very grand antique four-poster bed, beautifully decorated with hand-painted flowers and hung with Chinese silk curtains. The wallpaper was also hand-painted and depicted scenes from Chinese folklore. The decoration and furniture in the room dated back to the turn of the twentieth century, over a hundred years ago. It was a beautiful room, if a little faded in places, but that only added to its glamour. The day after the wedding the newlyweds would leave for a grand tour of Romania, or more precisely, a grand tour of Transylvania. A strange choice of destination for a honeymoon, but that's goths for you.

The Chinese bedroom would also be used by the bride-to-be to prepare herself and her wedding party for the wedding ceremony. The groom would be put in the blue bedroom at the end of the corridor overlooking the front lawns, a rather cold and dreary room despite the sun pouring in through windows on two sides. This was because no consideration had been given to insulation at the time the hall was built, more than a century ago, and this room had outside walls on the two sides that had windows. The windows and frames had warped over time and a draught blew in through the gaps all year round.

There were radiators in all the rooms at Threldale but they were not very efficient at heating up a room when switched on, and they did rattle noisily. This antiquated heating system was present in all the bedrooms, including the blue bedroom, in addition to an open fireplace. While the fire in this room would be lit every morning and kept stocked up with logs, it would only serve to warm the fireplace itself. I would not have liked to have slept in that room.

I cleaned, dusted, and vacuumed the extra rooms and put lots of clean white towels in the bathrooms. I also put bedside water flasks and posies of flowers in small vases in the bedrooms to cheer them up and make them a bit more welcoming.

As it was summer Lord Linton had turned the heating off to save money, so there was no point in my turning on any radiators. At least there would not be the noisy rattling to keep everyone awake at night. I did, however, make sure there were fires were laid in the fireplaces of all the rooms that had one, and that there were plenty of logs in the baskets. Soon everything was as ready as I could make it for the arrival of the happy couple.

The Honourable Alvin Crichton-Banks duly arrived, and his luggage was taken up by yours truly to the blue bedroom while he and Master Ted disappeared into the billiard room. I shivered as I placed his bags on the ottoman chest at the foot of the bed. Despite the warm day outside the blue bedroom was still cold so I had lit the fire earlier in the day, not that the room was any warmer as a result. My heart went out to the groom, having to sleep in this icebox.

'Better top up the fire,' I thought as I blew on my cold hands and put another couple of logs on the fire. The basket was full of enough logs to keep the fire going until late evening.

Two days later Miss Suzi Chambers arrived, and I took her and her bags up to the much more habitable Chinese bedroom. I had lit the fire in this room too, prior to the arrival of the bride-to-be, not that this room was anything like as cold as the blue bedroom. I placed the rather large garment bag, which I assumed contained the wedding dress, on the bed, and her cases on the chaise longue at the foot of the bed.

'I hope you don't mind,' she said, 'but I think my wedding dress may need a little attention. It got crushed in the back of the car on my way here. I did try to lie it flat on the back seat but it sort of slid off when I took a corner a bit too hard.' She pointed to the large garment bag on the bed.

'Not a problem. I will take it down to the laundry room and have a look,' I said, a little nervously. How do you give a wedding dress 'a little attention'? I picked up the garment bag, put it over my arm and left the room.

Once below stairs I took the garment bag into the laundry room down in the cellar, unzipped it and carefully lifted out the contents. I gasped as I looked at what the bride was going to wear for her big day. It was midnight blue – not a bad colour, if a little dark – and starched to be so stiff it made a sort of crinkling noise when the silk material moved. The skirt looked very long and narrow and had a fishtail. It would not be easy to walk in.

But that was not what had made me gasp. No, indeed. What had made me gasp was the number of fake – I hoped they were fake – cobwebs covering the fabric. They certainly gave the dress a macabre look, the like of which I had never seen before. I did what I could, gently pulling the dress into some sort of shape without pulling off any of the cobwebs. I was soon to learn that the midnight blue of the dress was to be the key colour theme of the big day.

I am not sure my attempts to straighten the dress made any difference, but I put it back into the garment bag and took it back up to the Chinese bedroom.

'Oh! You've done a wonderful job,' cooed Miss

Chambers as she took the dress out of the bag and held it up to the light streaming in through the window. At least someone was easy to please.

'I have been checking the rest of my outfit and I need some advice. Do you think my boots need a polish?' she asked, taking a pair of black Doc Martens out of her suitcase and holding them out to me.

'No, they look fine. Are they what you will be wearing with your dress?' I tried to sound like this was a normal question from a bride-to-be but I am not sure I succeeded.

'Yes, they are. I gave them a good polish before I packed them but I was worried they might have got scuffed in the case, but if you think they look all right then that's fine.'

At that point I pleaded pressure of work and left the room before my surprise at the choice of dress and footwear should become apparent to the bride. I dreaded to think what her veil and bouquet were like. It was going to be one of the strangest weddings I had ever seen.

The day before wedding the marquee was delivered and set up on the front lawns, complete with a solid floor for dancing at the end of the evening. Tables and chairs disappeared inside, along with lots of boxes of tablecloths, napkins, cutlery, crockery and other sundry items required for setting up a wedding breakfast.

I glanced through the windows of the marquee several times throughout the day. I watched the staff working on the various tables to change them from drab, plain wooden surfaces to beautiful white linen ones with midnight blue runners, set out with silver-plated cutlery and candelabras, crystal glasses, midnight blue napkins and pretty flower centrepieces. The chairs were dressed with white covers and tied with midnight blue ribbons. At least half a dozen large flower displays were taken into the marquee and put on stands in the corners. Despite my misgivings over the goth theme the marquee looked stunning by the end of the day.

The next day dawned warm and sunny, and from mid morning a steady stream of people began to arrive at the hall: caterers, the hairdresser, the florist, the photographer and Mr and Mrs Chambers, the parents of the bride. The wedding was scheduled to take place at 2 p.m. I had no additional duties to carry out so I was able to valet all the rooms and carry out my other duties in Threldale as I usually would.

Once I was done I kept out of the way in the Kitchen as much as I could. Even so, I still found myself running back and forth with trays of tea, coffee, biscuits and cake. First for the bridal party in the Chinese bedroom, Miss Suzi Chambers and her three bridesmaids, then for Mr and Mrs Chambers in the drawing room, who were chatting with Lady Linton. The groom's parents, Lord and Lady Crichton-Banks, were not arriving until just before the wedding. The groom and the best man had asked me to send up a couple of whiskies to the blue bedroom to help them relax. I took the liberty of including a plate of sandwiches to soak up the alcohol. I didn't want to be responsible for the groom turning up drunk at his own wedding.

As the hosts of the wedding location Lord and Lady Linton were not in the least bit relaxed. In fact they were a little bit flustered at having so many strangers wandering in and out of rooms all over their home. Lord Linton had taken refuge in the Library by 11.30 a.m., leaving Lady Linton, who was worried that something might go wrong, fussing around everyone.

By 12.30 p.m. things had calmed down, as everyone had either left or retired to their respective rooms to change into their wedding attire, so a hush descended on Threldale. Mr and Mrs Chambers had been given the garden room to use for the day. Lord and Lady Linton were in their own private suites. Muffled noises could be heard coming from the various bedrooms as the finishing touches were made to outfits and the results admired.

I cleared away the trays from the rooms and did a quick tidy-up and a plumping of cushions before going back to the Kitchen to wash up all the dirty dishes. As I was now surplus to requirements I grabbed a bite of lunch, and at 1.30 p.m. I walked up to the folly to watch events unfold.

Guests had started to gather and choose where they would sit or stand for the ceremony. There was no particular order specified by either the bride or the groom. They were a mix of young goths, dressed in black with startlingly pale faces and black eyeliner, and older people, more soberly dressed in the sort of outfits normally worn at a wedding. I decided to take up a position at the back, behind a broken wall, where I could still see what was going on.

I couldn't see Lord Linton at first but then I spotted him, wearing a dark suit with a white shirt, a pale blue cravat and a pale blue flower in his buttonhole. He was creeping around the outside of the folly with his head down, obviously hoping no one would waylay him and engage him in conversation. I am sure he would rather have been allowed to hide in the Library. He hated having to make small talk with complete strangers.

Lady Linton was easy to spot, in her pale blue chiffon dress with a delicate corsage of pale blue and white flowers pinned to it and a hat to match, as she moved among the guests chatting, smiling and enjoying seeing the grounds of Threldale Hall full of people. She appeared generally a lot more at ease than Lord Linton. I could clearly hear her from my vantage point.

'Yes, it is a lovely old hall.

'No, we aren't open to the public.

'Yes, it has always been owned by the same family.

'No, we aren't available for hire.

'The groom and my son have been friends since they were children. This is our wedding gift to him.

'Yes, it is a big responsibility, looking after Threldale.

'No, we run the whole place with very few staff.

'Yes, I find it a full time job running the house.

'No, only the bride and groom are staying with us.'

Lady Linton was obviously not missing me, so I remained where I was lurking behind a tumbledown wall out of sight.

The bride and groom had a glorious day for the wedding. But I had a strange feeling that, being goths, they would rather the sky was full of dark, brooding clouds in keeping with the gloomy surroundings. The air was warm and the sun shone out of a clear blue sky. There were only a few cotton wool clouds scudding high over the fells. The sunshine lit up the purple heather on the hilltops, and you could see the white blobs that were sheep grazing on the high ground. Days like these reminded me that this was a beautiful place to live.

At 1.30 p.m. I saw the Honourable Alvin Crichton-Banks leaving the house with Master Ted and walking across the lawns towards the folly. It took them about ten minutes. They took their time as they walked, chatting and laughing and totally relaxed. Both men looked resplendent in black outfits with white shirts and midnight blue cravats. Their black hair slicked back, black eyeliner, pale blue flowers in their buttonholes and pale faces recalled some Hammer horror movie from half a century ago. I was not sure that Master Ted was that comfortable with being dressed as a goth and having to wear make-up.

At 1.55 p.m. I looked back across the lawn, where I could see the bride leaving the hall with her wedding entourage, with what looked like a bouquet of dark blue, pale blue, purple and white flowers tied with a midnight blue ribbon. It was difficult to tell at that distance. While the bride had on her midnight blue silk bridal gown, the bridesmaids wore pale blue silk dresses. They all had pale faces, black eyeliner and blood-red lips, and were all wearing Doc Martens boots.

The bride had a pale blue lace veil held in place by a tiara decorated with lots of pearls. She was having to take lots of very small steps due to the narrow fit of her dress, and this looked all the more strange with her wearing Doc Martens. It was the strangest bridal procession I had ever seen. Due to the slow progress of the bride it was nearly 2.10 p.m. before they reached the folly and the ceremony could begin.

At this point my self-control finally gave up the fight and all I could think of was how ludicrous the bride, the groom and their entourage looked. If Christopher Lee were to give the bride away, Vincent Price to conduct the ceremony and vampire bats to fly in with the wedding rings I would not have been surprised. It was so far away from any other wedding I had seen that I found myself stifling a snigger, and so thought it would be better if I crept away from the folly and made my way back to the Kitchen inside Threldale.

Once inside I sat down and laughed until the tears ran down my face. It takes all sorts but this was the bride and groom's day, planned their way, and they did not need to have it spoilt by hearing me snorting with laughter in the undergrowth. I was able to spend the rest of the day watching all the wedding activities from my vantage point on the periphery.

After the service the photographer took lots of pictures of the bride and groom, sometimes with guests, sometimes without, all with that rictus smile beloved of wedding photographers. Waitresses came round with glasses of champagne, made a vivid red with the addition of crème de cassis, for the guests to drink while they waited around until they were needed for photographs or until they could congratulate the happy couple.

As for the reception, the caterers had the wedding feast well organised without needing any input from me. They even sent a large cold supper up to the hall for those who would be staying that night at Threldale. I busied myself with setting this up in the Dining Room before retiring to the Kitchen again to put my feet up with a cup of tea and a biscuit.

Although I didn't stay to see the wedding or have any involvement in the reception, I was informed by Lady Linton that the whole day went off without a hitch. The weather stayed dry, the ceremony was lovely, by all accounts, the food was good and the cake different. I say different because it was decorated in midnight blue and pale blue icing flowers with white icing cobwebs. It did have the statutory bride and groom figurines on top but I am surprised there was not a Dracula-style coffin somewhere on it as part of the decorations.

I went to bed that night a lot less exhausted than I usually was when there were lots of guests, but I found myself still giggling over what I came to think of as the *Hammer House of Horrors* wedding. Bela Lugosi eat your heart out!

The following day lots of people arrived very early (I was the only person up) to pack up all the trappings of the wedding feast back into the boxes they were unpacked from. The marquee was dismantled, the rubbish was picked up and put into black bin bags and the lawns were gradually cleared. The flower displays from the marquee were left on the table in the Entrance Hall. I would find places for them around the hall.

The happily married couple slept late into the morning, so Lady Linton asked me to take a breakfast tray up the Chinese bedroom just before midday. I loaded a tray with orange juice, coffee, toast, butter and marmalade, crockery and cutlery and headed up to the bedroom. I could hear giggling and whispering coming from the other side of the door. So, rather than disturb them by entering the room, I knocked and called out that there was a breakfast tray outside the door for them and scuttled back to the Kitchen, slightly embarrassed at having to take the tray up in the first place.

It was another couple of hours before the Honourable Alvin Crichton-Banks and his wife Mrs Suzi Crichton-Banks appeared downstairs with their suitcases packed, ready to leave on their honeymoon. A taxi came to pick them up from the front door ten minutes later.

Lord and Lady Linton waved off the happy couple and came back indoors. It had been an exciting few days, but it was time for a little peace and quiet at Threldale.

The Illegitimate Butler

*O*n a grey and cold morning time was moving on. The low clouds were obscuring the tops of the hills, making the dale feel closed off from the rest of the world.

Lady Linton was in the drawing room, sitting in an armchair close to a blazing log fire, a coffee tray close by, opening and reading her post when she suddenly stopped. She got up and came out into the Entrance Hall to call me from the cosiness of the Kitchen, where I was thinking about preparing lunch while cleaning the Aga. I took off my apron and made my way to the drawing room to find out what she wanted me for. I would have to come back and finish cleaning the Aga later.

'Ah, Rosie. I have an interesting letter here from the great-great-granddaughter of Blizzard, a butler who worked here for many years and retired to a cottage on the estate eighty years ago. Quite a surprise, don't you think?' Lady Linton smiled as she looked up from the letter she had been reading.

'Yes, Lady Linton. Very surprising,' I replied, a bit confused about why I would be surprised. I had no idea what came in her post. Plus I had never heard anyone mention any of the old butlers, never mind one called Blizzard. I thought it was a bit of a strange name, and it was not one that I had ever heard of before.

'Yes, it is. Blizzard has an interesting history with one of the previous earls. I have heard snippets from Lord Linton, but he doesn't like to talk about past indiscretions within the family,' continued Lady Linton.

I stood quietly, waiting for more information. This sounded like it might be a bit scandalous and everyone loves to hear a bit of scandal, including me. What was the indiscretion between a previous Earl Linton and Blizzard?

'Yes... Well, this letter gives more information on what happened at the time. The second son of one of Lord Linton's ancestors led one of the younger maids – a slip of a thing called Annie Blizzard – astray. It says here that she was only sixteen at the time. The silly girl found herself with child, which raised the prospect of a family scandal. Apparently it was all hushed up at the time.'

'Typical. Poor Annie,' I thought, but said nothing.

'The son was immediately bought a commission in the army and sent overseas. Annie was sent away somewhere suitable for unmarried mothers and had the child, a boy called Edward. A small allowance was then paid to Annie to allow her to raise the boy until he was old enough to come and work at Threldale. At the age of fourteen he came here to work as a bootboy, and over the years he rose to footman and finally butler. He was with the family for over sixty years, and when he retired he was allowed to live out his final days in a cottage in Hargrove. According to the letter he lived to the very respectable age of eighty-nine before passing away and being buried in the churchyard in Hargrove.' It wasn't like Lady Linton to be so expansive, so I did wonder where this was leading.

'What happened to Annie?' I asked, already guessing the answer. She would not have been given a second thought once her child had started work at Threldale Hall. I should imagine her allowance was stopped at that point too, poor woman. No job, no income and no son.

'No idea. The letter doesn't say,' said Lady Linton. 'Anyway, that is not the point of the letter. Miss Diana Blizzard has been researching her antecedents and now wishes to visit Threldale, the home of her great-great-grandfather, Edward Blizzard. With that in mind, I am going to invite Miss Blizzard and her family to lunch. I need you to prepare some sample lunch menus. Nothing too fussy. We will want to show them Threldale Hall at its best.'

With that she turned back to sorting out her post and ignored me. I considered myself dismissed and returned to the Kitchen to finish cleaning the Aga and planning what to make for lunch. My thoughts strayed to poor Annie Blizzard and her falling prey to one of the so-called gentry and then being blamed for getting pregnant. Even in our supposed modern times Lady Linton seemed to consider it Annie's own fault for her predicament.

Later on, once I had finished clearing away lunch and carrying out my remaining chores, I settled myself down at the table with a pen and a pad to give some thought to menus. All sorts of questions jostled in my head. What about vegan or vegetarian options? What about possible allergies or intolerances, such as nuts or gluten? How many courses would I need to do? How many people would there be? Would I be allowed to get in some help from the village? I knew I would be expected to answer these questions without bothering Lady Linton. As far as she was concerned I should be able to sort out these things out myself, so it was down to me to cover as many possibilities as I could when coming up with the menu options.

If help was needed at Threldale then it was totally reliant on the residents of the village coming to the rescue. There were two or three young ladies who had helped me out over the years, so hopefully I would be able to get hold of one of them to come up to the hall on the day of the lunch to give me a hand.

Between my normal household duties and answering the many calls of Lady Linton throughout the day, it was late afternoon before my drafts of two possible menus were complete and ready for her. I knew from previous experience of this nature that whatever I had suggested she would probably choose something completely different. I decided to leave it until the following morning before presenting them for her perusal, so I left them on the Kitchen table ready to take up to her when I was preparing breakfast.

The following morning I picked up the menus when I was taking up the milk, butter, jam and other items to the Dining Room and put them on the table ready for Lady Linton to look at when she came down. As it was she did not even glance at them, though she took them away with her after she had finished her breakfast.

A few days later, just when I thought she had forgotten all about the menus, I answered a summons to the drawing room in time to see her put the telephone down.

'That was Miss Blizzard confirming lunch,' said Lady Linton, turning around to talk to me. 'She and her family will be coming next Saturday. Now, I have looked at the menus and neither one is quite right for the lunch. However, I think we will have the French onion soup from the first menu and the salmon parcels from the second menu. I don't really like either dessert option, so I think we will have a nice light lemon mousse with some nice Scottish shortbread. We will take coffee and mints in the drawing room once we have finished lunch.'

I wasn't in the least surprised at the changes to the menu. It was pretty much what I expected to happen. At least she had chosen two of the courses from my suggestions.

'Yes, Lady Linton. How many will there be for lunch?' I enquired, hoping the number would be small, maybe half a dozen, and that Lady Linton would be relaxed enough to carry on answering my questions.

'Well, now, there will be Lord Linton and me, Miss Blizzard... Then I believe her parents, Mr and Mrs Blizzard, will be coming. I think she mentioned that she had two brothers who would be coming along. Now who else did she say? Let me think... Three or four cousins who are also interested in their ancestor, and I think she mentioned her partner would also be coming along.' I was trying to count as Lady Linton listed the attendees and I came to the grand total of eleven or twelve, depending on how many cousins came, not the small number I was hoping for.

'Will it be possible to get one of the young ladies from the village to help serve lunch?' I ventured hopefully. The young lady I had in mind would need to be paid for her time.

'Just to serve lunch yes, so for a couple of hours only. If you get everything properly organised then you should be able to manage for the rest of the time.' A couple of hours was better than nothing. It could have been worse. She could have said no.

I braced myself and asked the next question.

'Are there any special diets I need to cater for?'

'What? I don't know. I am sure if there were then Miss Blizzard would have mentioned it. You really need to sort these kinds of issues out yourself. I am far too busy to have to do your job for you.'

I think Lady Linton was getting a little bit tetchy with my questions, and I was surprised she had answered as many of my questions as she had. I beat a hasty retreat back to the Kitchen.

Over the next few days Miss Blizzard telephoned

a couple more times to discuss the lunch and who would be attending with her. As a result the numbers coming for lunch went down after the first call to six, and after the second call back up to the dizzying heights of thirteen. Bearing in mind that it had started at eleven or twelve, I was just going to have to plan for the worst and hope for the best. This seemed to be the case for most lunches or suppers Lady Linton invited friends or acquaintances to, so it was something I was used to.

The day of the lunch dawned. It was another day that was overcast and drizzling and not a day for showing off Threldale at its best, but typical of the dale we lived in. The hills around the dale were again shrouded in low cloud, hiding the tops of the surrounding hills.

I was up very early to start preparations. I planned to cater for fourteen sitting down to lunch and to split the menu to allow for twelve non-vegetarian and three vegetarian people lunching, which would include a spare serving in case another guest turned up unexpectedly. This meant making a second soup as the French onion soup included beef stock, which isn't very vegetarian. I chose asparagus, as that was quite quick and easy to do and would have a vegetable stock as a base. I already had a plentiful supply of home-made bread rolls, so that wasn't a problem.

I also needed a second main course, as an alternative to the salmon parcels, and opted for stuffed mushrooms, which were a bit fiddlier but still relatively easy and, like the salmon parcels, could be prepared ahead of time. Experience had taught me to be prepared for the unexpected, and hopefully that was what I had now done. The main course would be served with new potatoes and garden peas. Nice and simple. The dessert course was fine as it was, so long as no one had issues with dairy products. Now I felt a bit more comfortable with the menu options.

By the time Lord and Lady Linton came down to breakfast I had fourteen lemon mousse desserts – as requested by Lady Linton – made, put into glass dishes and setting in the pantry, I already had lots of home-made shortbread to go on the side of the dishes. I had made some avocado and goat's cheese canapés ready on serving plates, covered in cling film and also in the pantry. The French onion soup was made and simmering on the Aga. I would carry on with the preparations for the various courses after serving breakfast and completing my usual morning chores.

The guests were due to arrive at 12.30 p.m. Lady Linton would welcome them to Threldale and take them on a brief tour of the hall, followed by drinks and canapés in the drawing room. Lunch was to be served at 1.30 p.m. in the Dining Room. Lord Linton would join the lunch party for drinks and canapés. Prior to that he had estate business to discuss with Sam and Don. I think he just wanted to stay out of the way.

It was 11 a.m. before the Dining Room was vacated after breakfast, so it was then a rush to clear away the dirty dishes and set the room up for lunch. At least I had managed to get my other jobs done while waiting to get access to the room. I decided to set fourteen places and put two extra place settings in the cupboard under the serving table, just in case the numbers should rise.

Lady Linton was superstitious about numbers, so although there were thirteen for lunch an extra place had to be set to take the number up to fourteen. She used to refer to the fourteenth guest in these circumstances as Edward and had even been known, on occasion, to put one of Master Ted's childhood teddies in the vacant chair.

At 12.30 p.m. precisely the doorbell rang and I went to receive Lord and Lady Linton's guests. I opened the door to what seemed to be a sea of people. A young lady, wearing a red and white check jacket and with a red umbrella, separated herself from the others and introduced herself.

'Hello, I'm Diana, Diana Blizzard. I think we are expected.' She shook her brolly and folded it down.

'Yes, you are. Please come in. I will take you through to the drawing room, where Lady Linton is awaiting your arrival,' I replied as I stood to one side to let everyone in out of the drizzling rain. Once they were all in I showed them where they could divest themselves of hats, coats and umbrellas. One or two of them required the use of a bathroom to freshen up. It was a good five minutes before they were all ready for me to take them through to the drawing room and Lord and Lady Linton.

I had made a point of counting the number of people as they were coming in through the door, and was a bit surprised to find there were sixteen of them. I managed to attract Miss Blizzard's attention while everyone was still removing outer garments and sorting themselves out. I had a quick word with her just before she joined the rest of the guests to go into the drawing room.

'Will everyone be staying for lunch?' I asked.

'If that is all right. I know it's more than we agreed when I last spoke to Lady Linton, but as word got out other members of the family wanted to come along too. You don't mind, do you?' She sounded quite apologetic.

'Of course not. It isn't a problem. Please join the others.' This wasn't her problem. It was mine.

My mind raced as I wondered how I was going to handle the increase in numbers. I thought I had been clever by catering for fourteen, but the increase in numbers to sixteen proved that even my best-laid plans were not enough.

I opened the door to the drawing room and handed the guests over to the attentions of Lady Linton. While they were being shown the delights of the grander rooms of Threldale Hall I retrieved the extra two place settings and used them to set two extra places at the table in the Dining Room. Edward would not be needed today.

In the Kitchen I added extra beef stock to the French onion soup and extra vegetable stock to the asparagus soup. First course sorted. Next I made three more salmon parcels and stuffed another two mushrooms. I now had fourteen non-vegetarian and five vegetarian main courses. The dishes of new potatoes and garden peas were fine as they were. I had prepared plenty, so the increase in numbers wasn't an issue.

Dessert was more of a knotty problem. I had fourteen lemon mousses in the pantry and no backup plan. I scanned the pantry for inspiration. There on the top shelf was a single pack of twelve meringue nests. I checked the expiry date. They were fine. Next I checked the fridge to see what I had in the way of fresh fruit. There were two small punnets of strawberries in there that I had planned to use the next day in a fresh fruit salad, and a large carton of double cream. Strawberry and cream meringues! I breathed a sigh of relief, I could now serve a three-course lunch to sixteen people, complete with a vegetarian option and a choice of desserts.

My help with serving arrived at 1 p.m. in the person of Kylie Jenkins, the seventeen-year-old daughter of the village postman. She had stepped in to help me before, so she knew her way around Threldale. I would be able to just give her a job to do and she would get on with it without too much assistance from me. Also she would be on hand to help me until 3 p.m. I handed her an envelope containing the money we had agreed to pay her, because there might not be time later to give it to her.

The first job I got her to do was unwrap the canapés and take them through to the drawing room. Lady Linton would have finished taking her guests around

Threldale by then and would be offering them pre-lunch drinks. Once Kylie had returned to the Kitchen I got her to make up six strawberry and cream meringues, plate them up, cling film them and put them in the pantry with the lemon mousse desserts while I got on with the other courses. We were now good to go.

Now we were ready I sent Kylie back to the drawing room to help serving the canapés and the pre-lunch drinks. Lord and Lady Linton continued to entertain the guests with the history of the hall and the family who their ancestor, the butler Blizzard, had served during his sixty years of service. I wondered whether any mention would be made of his mother, the poor maid, Annie Blizzard, or of his father, the prodigal second son of Lord Linton's ancestor. Time went on and the proposed time for lunch of 1.30 came and went, as did 2 p.m.

At 2.05 p.m. Kylie appeared at the Kitchen door with a worried look on her face.

'I can stay on an extra half an hour after 3 p.m. but I have to leave by 3.30 p.m. at the latest. Do you think we will be done by then?' she asked.

'I hope so, but you go when you have to,' I replied. I knew Kylie had another job she had to get ready for after leaving Threldale, so I would just have to cope as best I could.

'OK, I'll let you know when I am leaving. Let's hope lunch has been served before then.' Kylie smiled and disappeared from the doorway to return to the drawing room serving drinks and canapés. We were both hoping Lady Linton would call everyone through for lunch soon.

Finally, at 2.15 p.m., Lady Linton sent Kylie back down to the Kitchen to say that everyone was ready for lunch to be served and could I 'pop out', as she wished to have a word with me. So I 'popped out' and hovered in the Entrance Hall as Lady Linton led her guests from the drawing room to the Dining Room and settled them around the table. I could see her pointing people at seats and doing her best to arrange them in some sort of order. She saw me waiting and came out to talk to me.

'Ah, there you are, Rosie. There are four vegetarians among our guests. I assume we do have a vegetarian option.'

'Yes, Lady Linton, we do.' I felt rather smug at my forward planning. I gave her details of the vegetarian options for the first and second courses and the additional choice for dessert, which she seemed happy with. She returned to the Dining Room and her guests and I returned to the Kitchen to get ready for service.

The next two hours were a blur of taking orders for either the vegetarian or non-vegetarian option, plating up, serving courses and clearing dishes. Kylie stayed on the extra half an hour as promised and left at 3.30 p.m. I battled on on my own and by 4.15 p.m. lunch was finally over. Lord and Lady Linton and their guests retired to the drawing room for coffee and mints. I was exhausted and the day was not yet over.

Both the Dining Room and the Kitchen were a mess.

I set to, clearing and cleaning the Dining Room, followed by a mountain of washing-up. I heard Lord and Lady Linton showing their guests out at 5.30 p.m. but didn't hear any summons for my presence, so I continued with the cleaning up. Finally, at 6.30 p.m., I was finished. I sat down for the first time with a cup of tea and stretched my aching feet out in front of me.

'Rosie!' I heard Lady Linton calling me as I had just got comfortable and was nodding off. I stood up, stretched my aching limbs and went to see what she wanted.

'Rosie, I think Lord Linton and I are a little tired now that our guests have gone. It has been a long afternoon. We will just have a light supper tonight. You can leave it in the Dining Room for us and take the rest of the night off.'

In all the rush of the day I hadn't given a thought to supper.

'No time to put my feet up yet,' I thought, as I made my way back to the Kitchen to rustle up a simple supper that I could leave in the Dining Room. There wouldn't be much of a night off for me to take.

The Annual Trustee Meeting

$\mathcal{L}$ike a lot of the stately homes still in the hands of the original families, Threldale Hall was held in trust. One of the conditions of the trust was that there had to be annual trustee meetings. One or two had been held at Threldale during the many years I had been there but they were always extra work, preparing tea and coffee trays, catering for extra places at mealtimes and sometimes setting up guest rooms for some of the trustees.

Sometimes some of the trustees would stay on for a few days, taking in the delights of Threldale and its dale. As the meeting was usually held in summer, afternoon tea could be taken on the front lawn after business had been concluded, looking down the dale in the general direction of Hargrove or looking up to the heather-clad hilltops.

Thankfully, from my point of view, the meetings were more often than not held elsewhere, depending on the other commitments of the trustees attending. Sometimes these meetings were held in London at the home of Lord Linton's sister, Mrs Kingsley-Grey, and sometimes they were held at the home of the Honourable Albert Linton, Lord Linton's cousin, a trustee who lived in Cumbria. There had been a few years when they were held in Leeds in a hotel conference room organised by Mr Charles Digby-Harcourt, Lord Linton's solicitor, a trustee who travelled up from London. This last option had proved to be the least stressful but was considered to be rather extravagant, as hotels could be expensive. Threldale was not in a position to squander money.

The location depended on where it was most convenient for the trustees to get to when the time for the meetings came around. This summer it was to be at Threldale, at the request of Lord and Lady Linton.

The year before it had been in London at the home of the Kingsley-Greys, a large flat of spacious proportions in Knightsbridge. To attend the meeting Lord and Lady Linton had travelled down to London on the train from York the day before, stayed overnight at the Kingsley-Greys, attended the trustee meeting and immediately afterwards caught a train back to York, arriving back at Threldale very late in the evening, tired and travel-weary.

In previous years, when the meeting had been in London, they had stayed with the Kingsley-Greys for a lot longer, but in cutting the trip back to just two days they had found the whole experience exhausting. So the decision to have it at Threldale this year had been made by them, as they did not want to travel anywhere.

The trustees coming to this year's meeting included Mr George and Mrs Thomasina (known to the family as Tommy) Kingsley-Grey, who were Lord Linton's brother-in-law and sister, the Hon. Albert Linton, who was Lord Linton's first cousin, Mr Charles Digby-Harcourt, and finally Lord and Lady Linton themselves. So there would be six people attending as trustees.

There was talk of maybe inviting Master Ted as a non-participating attendee, to prepare him for the day when he would become one of the trustees. By all accounts, though, that would not be for a few years yet, as his priorities at the moment were his law studies up at Oxford. Another factor was his age. Being a young man in his twenties, he didn't have any great interest in the running of the Threldale estate and hall.

Several months prior to this year's meeting the date and time had been organised as 10 a.m. on the second Friday in August, and it was agreed that the location for the meeting was to be the Library at Threldale Hall. The trustees travelling to Threldale were due to arrive between 8 a.m. and 9 a.m. on the day of the meeting, in time for an early breakfast provided by yours truly, before getting started. I was told to have everything set up in the Dining Room by 8.15 a.m., ready for the arrival of the trustees.

To get to the meeting on time Mr and Mrs Kingsley-Grey were catching an early flight from London to Leeds-Bradford Airport and then getting a taxi out to the hall. The Hon. Albert Linton was driving over from his home in Cumbria. Mr Digby-Harcourt was coming up by train from London two days before the trustee meeting, as he had some other business to transact in Leeds, and he would be driving himself to Threldale in a hire car. Master Ted would already be at home from university for the summer recess, but there was still some question over whether he would attend the meeting.

What could possibly go wrong?

On the day of the meeting I had the Dining Room set up, as requested, by 8.15 a.m. for a hearty breakfast consisting of bacon, sausages, mushrooms, tomatoes, scrambled eggs, toast, orange juice and coffee. A good solid selection, which should fill the trustees up until lunchtime.

Lord and Lady Linton were down at 8.45 a.m., followed by Master Ted at 9 a.m. The three of them settled down to breakfast and awaited the arrival of the other four trustees. Barring any unforeseen circumstances it was looking like the meeting should begin on time at 10 a.m.

That was not to be.

The time of the meeting arrived but there was no sign of any of the other trustees. At 10.30 a.m. the house phone rang, to be answered by Lady Linton. From what I could hear from her side of the conversation it was Mrs Kingsley-Grey, Lord Linton's sister.

'Hello, Threldale Hall. Lady Linton speaking.

'Tommy, where are you? The meeting was supposed to start half an hour ago.

'You've missed the flight. What do you mean? You misread the flight time and arrived an hour too late? You must have checked the tickets, Tommy.

'You are on the next one, so what time do you think you will get here?

'Not until after lunch!

'Well, we will just have to wait until you get here.

'Bye for now, Tommy. We will see you this afternoon.' Lady Linton hung up the phone with a sigh.

She went back into the Dining Room to inform Lord Linton of events. There was still no sign of either the Hon. Albert Linton or Mr Digby-Harcourt. The morning moved on, while the breakfast slowly congealed in the chafing dishes in the Dining Room. At Lady Linton's request, Lord Linton disappeared into the Library to make some phone calls regarding the missing trustees. He reappeared fifteen minutes later looking for Lady Linton.

'Where are you, dear?'

'In the drawing room.' Lady Linton called him from the sofa where she was drinking coffee and reading the morning paper.

'I have managed to speak to Bertie. You will not believe this. He was still at home. He has the meeting down in his diary for tomorrow. More than that, he can't come today as he has a funeral to go to at lunchtime in Kendal. Unbelievable.'

'What do you mean, a funeral?'

'Yes, dear, the funeral of an old friend from his university days. He thought the meeting and the funeral were on different days. He says if we can put the meeting back to late afternoon he might just be able to make it. I said I will call him back when I know a time for the meeting.'

'This is ridiculous. What about Charles? Did you call him?'

'Patience, patience, dear. Let a chap finish telling a tale. Yes, I called Charles on his mobile. He's been delayed by an urgent bit of business arising out of a meeting he had yesterday with a client in Leeds. Apparently it couldn't wait. It needs to be sorted out before he drives up here. He will get to Threldale as soon as he can.'

So it looked like none of the other trustees were going to make it for breakfast, not that any of it was still edible. I waited until Lord Linton had left the drawing room and returned to the Library. Then I had a quick word with Lady Linton.

'Shall I clear away breakfast, Lady Linton?' I asked.

'I suppose so. Can you rustle up a late lunch for six? Hopefully we will eat around 2 p.m. We will have to move the trustee meeting until the middle of the afternoon.'

'Yes, Lady Linton.' I left her to finish reading the morning paper and headed for the Dining Room.

I blew out the tea lights under the chafing dishes and cleared away the now spoilt breakfast. There was an awful lot of it left. I had catered for seven and only three had eaten. Lady Linton does not like waste and neither do I. If I froze the bacon and sausages I could probably chop them up and put them in a quiche at a later date. I could whizz the toast in the food processor to make breadcrumbs and put that in the freezer too. Just about everything else – the eggs, the tomatoes and the mushrooms – would have to go in the bin.

Next I cleaned the Dining Room and set the table up for lunch for six. I had already planned the lunch, so I just needed to make sure it was ready for 2 p.m. I had roasted a ham the day before so I would slice that and serve it with a green salad, a caprese salad, a potato salad and some bread rolls. It would just be fruit, cheese and crackers to follow. I hoped it was enough, because I had banked on everyone having a big breakfast. I would put coffee and plenty of home-made biscuits in the Library, where it was planned to hold the trustee meeting, if the other trustees ever arrived for it. So far it wasn't looking promising.

Once I had it all prepared there was not a lot else I could do except wait with Lord and Lady Linton for the arrival of the missing trustees. I took a tea tray up to the drawing room at 11.30 a.m., more to pass the time than because anyone had asked for it. It was lucky that I had some mending I could be getting on with at the Kitchen table while I waited.

At midday, just as I went to collect the tea tray from the drawing room, the telephone rang again and Lady Linton answered it, probably hoping for good news from one of the trustees. I took my time removing the tray so that I could hear what was said.

'Hello, Threldale Hall. Lady Linton speaking.

'Tommy, I thought you were on a flight!

'What do you mean you can't get on the flight?

'You forgot your passports and they won't let board without proof of identity documents.

'How stupid! No, not you, Tommy. The airline.

'What are you going to do now?

'George is having the passports sent over to the airport from the flat. Does your housekeeper know where to find them?

'She does. Thank goodness for that, at least.

'Well, it can't be helped. When do you hope to get here?

'About 4 p.m. We will see you then.'

She went to find Lord Linton in the Library and give him the latest information regarding his sister and her husband. I was beginning to wonder if Mr and Mrs Kingsley-Grey would ever arrive. There were still doubts over whether the Hon. Albert Linton would be able to make after he had attended the funeral.

So far the day had been a farce. Around 12.30 p.m., just when I wondered what would go wrong next, the front doorbell rang. Lady Linton went to answer it and there stood Mr Digby-Harcourt, one of the missing trustees. She welcomed him like a long-lost friend and took him into the drawing room to recover from his drive up to Threldale from Leeds. At least there would be four people for lunch at 2 p.m. Finally, things were starting to look better for the meeting.

It now looked likely, if the Kingsley-Greys arrived as planned after getting a taxi from the airport, that the meeting was not going to take place until 4.30 p.m. at the earliest. Lord Linton called the Hon. Albert Linton back and asked if he could possibly get to Threldale from Kendal for that time. He couldn't, unless it was a little bit later than that. So it was agreed to push the meeting back to 5 p.m. by which time, hopefully, all the other trustees would have arrived.

Lunch was served at 2 p.m. to Lord and Lady Linton, Master Ted and Mr Digby-Harcourt, and passed without incident. There were no more phone calls, incoming or outgoing. I put the tray of coffee and home-made biscuits in the drawing room (instead of the Library, as I had planned, if the meeting had gone ahead in there) and left them to it. We were all now waiting for Mr and Mrs Kingsley-Grey to arrive by taxi from the airport and for the Hon. Albert Linton to arrive in his car from Cumbria.

I cleared away lunch from the Dining Room, cleaned it and gave the table a quick polish. Now that lunch was over there was an option to use either that room or the Library for the trustee meeting. To my mind the Dining Room was the better option, having a large table for all the trustees to sit round, but previous meetings had been held in the Library, with its large desk and comfortable armchairs.

There were no further phone calls throughout the afternoon, so it looked like the meeting might actually go ahead at 5 p.m. However, by 4.30 p.m. there was still no sign of the Kingsley-Greys and I could see Lady Linton pacing up and down the drawing room, worried that, after all the delays and rescheduling, the meeting might still not go ahead.

With just fifteen minutes to go before before the rescheduled time for the meeting the front doorbell rang. It was answered by a rather flustered Lady Linton. On the doorstep were the three missing trustees: Mr and Mrs Kingsley-Grey, finally having made it on to a flight from London to Leeds-Bradford, and the Hon. Albert Linton, having driven over from Cumbria after attending the funeral in Kendal.

'You made it! Tommy, George, I thought you'd missed another flight. Bertie, so sorry to hear about your friend. It was good of you to still come. Come through to the drawing room.' Lady Linton sounded relieved that all the trustees were finally present.

'Rosie, we'll have coffee and biscuits in the drawing room.'

I hurried down to the Kitchen and made up what I hoped was the last coffee tray of the day, this time for seven people, as Master Ted would be attending the meeting after all. I took the tray up and noticed Lady Linton closing the Library door.

'We will be using the Dining Room, Rosie. Put the coffee tray on the table in there.'

I entered quietly and put the tray on the table. The other trustees were already settling themselves down on chairs around the table and arranging pens and paper in front of them. I went out just as quietly as I came in and left them to their trustee meeting, at last.

I expected the meeting to go on for quite a few hours so I made up a supper of chicken and vegetable soup in an insulated flask, a salmon and asparagus quiche, and a couple of large plates of egg and cress sandwiches, which I would take up around 8 p.m. and they could help themselves. I also nipped upstairs and set up two of the guest bedrooms – the Chinese bedroom and the blue bedroom – and then I came back down and set up the garden bedroom on the ground floor. I put towels in the bathrooms, turned on the hot water and placed drinking water flasks and glasses on the bedside tables, just in case they were needed.

The meeting did indeed go on for hours. I took up the supper as I had planned at 8 p.m., including plates, napkins and cutlery, all of it loaded on to an old-fashioned hostess trolley. I also took in a jug of home-made lemonade with some tumblers and wine glasses. I assumed everyone had consumed enough coffee during the day. If they wanted something stronger, such as a glass or two of wine, Lord Linton would be the person to see to that requirement.

I spent most of the rest of the time, while the meeting was going on, in the Kitchen, popping out to the Entrance Hall every now and then to see if it was still going on. The meeting finally closed at 9.30 p.m., at which point I went into the Dining Room and was pleased to see the light supper had gone down well. The soup flask was empty, as were the plates of sandwiches. There were a couple of slices of quiche left but that was all. Lord Linton had indeed been into the wine cellar and had provided a couple of bottles of white wine to help wash supper down.

The trustees retired to the drawing room to relax with the last of the white wine. The Hon. Albert Linton and Mr Digby-Harcourt had both stuck with the home-made lemonade. At 10 p.m. the Hon. Albert Linton stated that it was time he left. He would drive back to Cumbria the same night. It had been a long and busy day for him, having to attend a funeral in one county and a trustee meeting in a different

131

county. He was tired and just wanted to return to his own home, and by leaving so late it would probably be close to midnight before he got there.

Being a solicitor with important appointments to keep, Mr Digby-Harcourt would leave at the same time. He had an express train to catch the next morning from Leeds to London, so he drove back to Leeds to stay overnight in the same hotel he had used for the previous couple of nights, ready for the early departure the following morning.

Mr George and Mrs Thomasina Kingsley-Grey decided they would stay the night at Threldale before getting a taxi back to the airport to fly home to London the next day. They settled themselves in armchairs in the drawing room with the remains of the white wine and caught up on family matters with Lord and Lady Linton and Master Ted.

I nipped back upstairs and switched off the lights and the hot water in the blue bedroom and went back down and did the same in the garden bedroom, but left the Chinese bedroom ready to be used by Mr and Mrs Kingsley-Grey. There was nothing else I could do that evening, so I informed Lady Linton that I was retiring and she wished me goodnight.

I sincerely hoped that next year's meeting would be held in Leeds, London or Cumbria. Anywhere but Threldale. I was not sure that I, never mind Lord and Lady Linton, would be able to handle the disruption to the normal routine.

Cataloguing the Library

Lord and Lady Linton believed themselves to be the custodians of Threldale Hall, not just the owners. They believed it was their duty to, at the very least, preserve the house and its contents and, at best, pass on the custodianship to the next generation with the house in better shape than when they inherited it. This also went for the estate grounds, the houses in Hargrove village and the local farms that fell within their stewardship.

This was an ongoing task as there were many outbuildings on the estate to look after, and in the village there were at least two dozen cottages. Then there were the hill farms with their farmhouses, barns and sheds. In fact across the dale there were a lot of maintenance responsibilities, and they had to be prioritised according to need and finances. This meant that jobs at Threldale Hall may wait for years or even decades before reaching the top of the list.

With this list of priorities in mind, Lord Linton decided it was time to recatalogue the contents of the Library as it was many decades since it had last been done, and it therefore needed doing as a matter of urgency. There were hundreds of books filling the shelves, and some of them were so fragile that they were wrapped in a special tissue paper and bound with protective ribbon.

Some of the books were quite rare and valuable and some were not, but this was not reflected in the old catalogue. Besides the books there were also also countless documents, plans and items of old correspondence cluttering Lord Linton's large mahogany desk, which occupied a large space in front of the window looking out over the estate grounds. Some of these items needed to be catalogued and filed along with the books.

The previous catalogue must have been put together at least fifty years ago, if not longer. I had seen it in an old Manila folder perched precariously on the edge of Lord Linton's desk among a pile of letters, newspapers and books, just waiting to be misplaced. Being a conscientious housekeeper, I had taken the opportunity to put it away in a safer place, a document box on one of the few empty shelves. At the time I had told Lord Linton where I had put it, but I don't think he took much notice of what I said. But at least I knew it was safe, should he ever ask for it.

As cataloguing was quite a specialist task an advertisement was placed in the relevant periodicals for a temporary position as librarian to come to work at Threldale Hall for six months to carry out the huge task of cataloguing the entire contents of the Library. The successful applicant would have to live within a commutable distance and be able to drive, due to the isolated location of the dale the hall sat in. The nearest large town was a good hour's drive away (although there were nearer small communities), so whoever it was came to do the job would have to either already live quite close by or be prepared to move closer for the duration of the contract.

Several applicants came for interviews with Lord Linton. I would let them in at the front door and take them through to the Library, and after around an hour I would let them out again. I didn't get to talk to any of them, so I had no idea who they were or how they had got on during their interviews. Lord Linton did not even offer those attending interviews tea or coffee, so I wasn't required to take a tray into the Library at any time. It must have made for a difficult interview for the prospective librarians. I think he should at least have made sure there was a glass of water on offer. The interviewees must have got thirsty while having to discuss the requirements of the job and answer questions.

Once all those selected to come and see Lord Linton had been interviewed, he dispatched a letter offering the position to the successful applicant. The job was accepted and I awaited his or her arrival. I thought it would be nice to have some new blood about the place and looked forward to meeting the new member of house staff, even if it was only temporary. Having dusted the books in the Library every year for the last ten years I was sure I would be able to offer some small assistance to whoever was appointed and, more importantly for me, I would have someone else to talk to.

At 9 a.m. sharp on a Monday morning, a few weeks after the position had been filled, the front doorbell rang and I opened the door to a man who I would guess to be in his early thirties, a good deal younger than me anyway. Lord Linton had warned me the previous day that the new librarian was to start on the Monday and that I was to look after him and get him settled in.

'Hello, my name is Stefan Linklater. I am Lord Linton's new librarian. I am to start cataloguing the contents of the Library. I start today and I am supposed to report to Lord Linton. I've left my car parked outside on the drive. Will it be all right there? Do I need to park it somewhere else?'

'Yes, it'll be fine there. Lord Linton is expecting you. Please come in and I'll take you through to the Library and get you settled in.' I stood to one side to allow him to come in.

'I am a bit nervous. This is my first job cataloguing a private Library. Up until now I have only worked in public libraries, which is completely different to this. I am fully qualified, but Lord Linton knows that. Will he come to the Library when he is ready to see me? Do you know where I am supposed to start?' He was a little pink, and fiddled constantly with a black leather folder he was holding against his chest.

I decided that the first thing I needed to do was get him into the Library and try and make him feel more at home. We walked across the Entrance Hall and I opened the door to the Library for him to go in first. Once inside he took his coat off and put it over the back of an armchair. I told him to settle himself in the leather office-type chair behind the mahogany desk in front of the window and usually occupied by Lord Linton. I was sure that Lord Linton wouldn't mind, as Mr Linklater needed a desk to work at.

'I am sorry, but Lord Linton hasn't breakfasted yet. I am sure he will come to the Library when he is ready. In the meantime just make yourself at home in here. I'll hang your coat up in the Entrance Hall,' I said, lifting it off the armchair and taking it with me.

'Thank you. I'll go ahead and make a start by familiarising myself with the Library. I am so nervous about working with Lord Linton and making a good job of cataloguing these lovely old books. Is there a bathroom I can use? And is there somewhere I can get a glass of water?'

'No problem. And just relax. Lord Linton doesn't bite. Follow me and I will show you the staff loo and the Kitchen, where you can make as many drinks as you want and where you can have lunch. Once you are comfortable and back in the Library I'll bring you a coffee tray and a few biscuits to tide you over until Lord Linton appears.' He seemed to be quite a nice young man. I thought I was going to like him being around once he relaxed a bit.

I took the promised tray into the Library with a pot of hot coffee, a couple of cups and saucers and a plate of biscuits, then left him to sort himself out and await the arrival of Lord Linton. I didn't see either of them throughout the morning so I assumed the two of them had got down to work in the Library. I did go in to retrieve the coffee tray just before midday, and they both had their heads down over some document or other on the desk. I put everything back on the tray as quietly as I could and left them to it, taking the tray back to the Kitchen with me.

For my part, I spent the rest of the morning carrying out my duties as usual, but Lady Linton tracked me down cleaning the banisters on the main staircase.

'Rosie, we will be three for lunch today. As it is his first day with us Mr Linklater will be joining Lord Linton and me.'

'Yes, Lady Linton.' I felt sorry for Mr Linklater having to eat with his boss on his first day. The poor man was nervous enough without having to make small talk over lunch.

'He and Lord Linton seem to be getting on well. It is a big task, cataloguing all the books. It will keep Lord Linton occupied for a few months.'

'Yes, Lady Linton.'

She turned away, leaving me to finish cleaning the banisters. My life is just one glorious round of exciting household chores.

At lunchtime I set an extra place for Mr Linklater. There was plenty to go round, so that wasn't a problem. Today I had prepared chicken and mushroom pasta in a fresh basil pesto sauce with salad and garlic bread. I had set up a board with cheese, crackers and fresh grapes to follow. I put the pasta in a warm chafing dish and set the rest out on the sideboard ready for them to help themselves. I hoped his nerves had subsided by lunchtime and he would be relaxed enough to eat. He and Lord Linton seemed to get on well, but would he get on with Lady Linton equally well?

I thought no more about it until I saw Lady Linton later that afternoon.

'Rosie, we had a bit of a problem at lunchtime. It would appear that Mr Linklater is a little bit clumsy. He dropped some of his pasta on the floor, and I have never seen anyone have so much trouble eating a salad. You will need to clean up the mess he made on the floor.' She sounded a bit put out.

'Yes, Lady Linton.'

'He seemed to cope with the cheese and biscuits a little better. If I didn't know any better I would have thought the man was of a nervous disposition.'

'Yes, Lady Linton.' My heart went out to Mr Linklater. He probably hadn't expected he would have to eat with his employers on his first day. I know I would feel uncomfortable lunching with them even after working for them for the last ten years.

'Lord Linton invited him for lunch today but I do hope the invitation will not be repeated. I found the man rather tiring. It would seem his only topic of conversation is books.'

'Yes, Lady Linton.' I think I would have struggled to find a suitable subject for conversation over lunch, so I wasn't surprised that he had defaulted to a subject he knew and understood.

I cleared away lunch and gave the carpet a bit of a clean where Mr Linklater had been sitting. It was a bit of a mess. It looked like the poor man had trodden in the pieces of pasta after he had dropped them. He was probably hoping the lunch invitation wouldn't be repeated as well.

Each day over the next few mornings the front doorbell would ring, I would let Mr Linklater in, and we would have a quick conversation while he hung up his coat before he headed for the Library. He already knew where to find the things to make a cup of tea or coffee and where the biscuit tin was and he got into a routine, where he would come through to the Kitchen ten minutes after arriving to make himself a mug of coffee and grab a couple of biscuits to take up to the Library with him. Once fortified with caffeine and sugar he would begin work for the day poring over the books, plans, documents, old correspondence, lists and any notes left by Lord Linton.

Apart from that we only saw each other over lunch in the Kitchen, or if I happened to be there when he refreshed his mug of coffee. I had offered to provide lunch for him each day but he preferred to bring in his own sandwiches. Lord Linton would pop in and out of the Library throughout the day, offering him advice, making suggestions or just trying to offer help with the cataloguing, not that he quite understood what Mr Linklater was doing.

As for any further lunch invitations, Lord Linton was under instructions from Lady Linton not to repeat the initial offer. Mr Linklater spent his lunchtimes either on his own in the Library or with me in the Kitchen, depending on what he was working on, how cold he was feeling and whether or not he just wanted a friendly face to talk to. The Library could get quite chilly. The heating was rarely on in there as it would dry the books, and as the Aga was permanently on the Kitchen was always warm and welcoming.

By the start of the second week I was a bit curious about how things were progressing. I had no idea what was involved in cataloguing a Library. Stefan – not Mr Linklater any longer. We were now on first-name terms – came in, worked hard, kept Lord Linton informed, and at the end of the day went home again.

My curiosity was about to be satisfied. Lord Linton made a comment to me at breakfast, when I took him his fresh pot of coffee, that Mr Linklater wanted a word with me about catalogues. I decided to go straight across to the Library to find out what Stefan wanted, though I thought it a bit strange that he hadn't mentioned anything when he arrived that morning.

'Ah, Rosie, I had a question for Lord Linton yesterday that he couldn't answer. He says you are the person who may be able to answer it. I didn't want to ask you directly in case I would be disturbing you.' I waited with anticipation. What did I know that Lord Linton didn't?

'I need the last catalogue, which was drawn up several decades ago. I have been told you are probably the only person who knows where it is.' Lord Linton was right. I knew he hadn't been listening when I told him where I had put it. The folder containing the last catalogue was in a document box on one of the lesser-used shelves in the Library.

'So can you tell me where it is, then?' Stefan was looking at me strangely, and I realised I was just standing there grinning like a Cheshire cat.

'Sorry, of course I can. Just a minute,' I said, and walked over to one of the bookshelves behind the desk and knelt down and took the document box from the shelf. Inside was an old brown folder tied up with a black ribbon.

'The last catalogue.' I handed it to Stefan.

'Thank you so much for this. I had looked in every drawer and on every shelf. I never thought of looking in any of the document boxes. How stupid of me.' And with that he turned back to his desk and undid the ribbon excitedly.

'Anything else?' I asked.

'No, but I know who to ask the next time I have a question Lord Linton can't answer,' he said, and laughed.

I nearly skipped out of the Library. It made a change from cooking, cleaning and laundry duties.

Another week passed without Stefan needing any help from me, and again I was getting curious. Just like the previous week, Lord Linton indicated that Mr Linklater wished to talk to me, and so I went straight to the Library to see what Stefan wanted this time.

'You wanted to ask me something? You can ask me directly, you know. Neither Lord nor Lady Linton will mind if you do. In fact they would probably prefer it if you asked me first. I am more likely to know where something is in this house than either one of them,' I said, closing the Library door behind me. I was keen to help in any way.

'Thank you, Rosie, I'll try and remember that. For now, though, I have a problem. Not all the books are where the old catalogue says they should be. Some of the books seem to be missing from the shelves where they are supposed to be. I assume that as the fount of all knowledge here at Threldale you know where they are, or at least where I can find them.'

This one was easy to sort out.

'Lord Linton rarely puts books back where he gets them from, usually because he can't remember, so he will put them back on any shelf that happens to have a space. He has also been known to take them with him when he leaves the Library and just abandon them on some random surface that he passes. I often find them in other rooms around the house. At least once a week I go round the house collecting them up and putting them on the desk in here. Now and again I try and put the growing pile back on the shelves where they belong.'

'That sounds really frustrating for you.'

'Not a bit. Lord Linton is just not always aware of where he has put a book down. I thought it prudent that one of us should know the whereabouts of the books that have not been returned to their catalogued place, and as he can be a little forgetful I decided that person should be me. It is more likely to be frustrating for you trying to catalogue books and finding Lord

143

Linton has moved them.' I smiled.

'So, Rosie, are you trying to tell me that you know this Library better than Lord Linton?' He looked at me with something approaching respect.

'Not necessarily, but I have found it useful to have a sharper memory. Now, could you do with me helping you out for an hour this morning?' I asked hopefully.

'If you know where the missing books are then, yes, I definitely want your help.'

'Good. Then shall we press on?'

We spent the next hour going through the various questions he had about the missing or misplaced books and the best way to go about locating them. By the end of that time I think Stefan was in a much better position regarding finding the missing items, and was able to continue with the cataloguing without any further help from me.

Each morning, over the following five months, I would open the front door to Stefan. He would wish me 'Good morning,' hang up his coat and go into the Library. He would make himself a coffee and begin his work. While in the Library he would keep himself supplied with coffee and biscuits at regular intervals throughout the day or he would come through to the Kitchen to have a cuppa and warm himself in front of the Aga.

With only a couple of weeks to go until the end of his contract he had all the information he needed, and he was ready to collate all his findings into a new catalogue to present to Lord Linton.

I would like to be able to say that during this time the relationship between Lady Linton and Stefan Linklater improved, but that was not to be the case. She continued to find him tiring and clumsy, and avoided engaging him in conversation if she should see him at all during his working day. He, for his part, found Lady Linton a lot less approachable than Lord Linton so he stayed in the Library as much as possible, except when he managed to escape to the Kitchen.

The final day of Stefan's contract finally arrived. He made a grand presentation of the new catalogue to Lord Linton that was printed on crisp white quality paper, ring-bound with hardcovers front and back, and with a pocket inside containing a computer disc holding the same information, should further copies need to be printed. Neither Lord or Lady Linton owned a computer, so they weren't sure what to do with a computer disc. At some point in the near future I would retrieve it from the binder and store it elsewhere.

To produce the master disc copy Stefan had used his own laptop, which he had brought to work with him each day over the last month. He had used the disc to get the printed copy done at a printer's in Leeds. Should both the disc and the printed copy go missing he would still have the original on his laptop.

A couple of days before this grand presentation I had had a quiet word with Stefan regarding Lady Linton and how he might leave Threldale in her good books. So, on that last day, he thanked her for her hospitality over the last six months and gave her a rather beautiful bouquet of flowers with a hand-painted thank-you card. She had the grace to blush.

It had been an interesting six months, and I had enjoyed assisting Stefan over that time. It had proved to be a welcome distraction from my normal duties. I had also enjoyed having company in my Kitchen and someone to talk to who wasn't connected to Threldale.

Jingle Bells

In the grounds of Threldale Hall, round the back of the hall in a cobbled courtyard, there was an old stable block that dated back to the days when the only transport available relied on horses. This stable block had not only stalls for the horses but also a large open carriage bay for storing the various carriages and carts that would have transported the Linton family around the area.

There were all sorts of other outbuildings on the estate, comprising an old laundry building and an old workshop in the same courtyard as the stable block, a gamekeeper's cottage over on the far side of the estate close to woodland and a smithy complete with its own forge. All of them were slowly crumbling into decay and dereliction.

The stable block had not been used since the demise of the need for horse-drawn vehicles. It was history frozen at a particular point in time and it still contained the stalls, complete with the names of the horses that had been stabled in them on plaques on the wall at the back of the stalls. No horses could have been stabled in those stalls now. They were piled high with junk, old mattresses, sofas, beds, chairs and other unwanted pieces of furniture, slowly rotting away where they had been left or dumped depending on your point of view. I would say 'dumped', but Lady Linton would say, 'carefully stored for future use'.

The open carriage bay held a four-seat state coach, complete with the family coat of arms hand-painted on to the doors and with horsehair-stuffed and leather-upholstered seating inside for four people. The windows of the carriage had the remnants of silk curtains hanging on the inside in dilapidated tatters. The glass windows themselves could be opened or closed, using a leather strap that supported the window frame.

There was also a two-seat brougham with similar leather upholstery stuffed with horsehair, but without the coat of arms and silk curtains. Both carriages were more than a century old, dated from the days before petrol-driven cars, and had not been used since those times. Along with the two carriages there was a sleigh from a time when winters were cold and meant lots of snow. All three vehicles showed the signs of years of neglect.

The huge double doors that opened out revealing the carriage bay were rotten and crumbling at the bottom, and as a result anything and everything would blow under the doors throughout the year. The stable block had not been maintained for many years, so the amount of rubbish blowing under the doors had just accumulated with the passing of time. At the back of the bay there were piles of leaves and twigs at least three feet high, and the rest of the floor space was covered in a little under a foot of debris. Luckily the doors opened outwards, so that this accumulation of muck did not impede their function in any way.

Because the state coach and the brougham were hooded and enclosed they had been spared the build-up of this blown-in detritus getting inside the carriages. However, the same could not be said of the external condition of either of them. They were covered in a thick layer of dust, which was overlaid with twigs, leaves and cobwebs. Despite this sad state of affairs it was obvious to anyone seeing them that they had both once been a very grand and imposing sight. It would have been a spectacle to see members of the Linton family out in either one of them, being pulled along by well-fed horses whose coats shone with good health.

The sleigh, sadly, was in a very sorry state, though it too had once been a very grand affair. It was difficult to see its glory under the pile of leaves and twigs that almost buried it. The sleigh was drawn by a single horse and could hold two people on leather-upholstered seating, who could snuggle up under blankets and furs against the worst effects of the cold. The reins that would lead from the sleigh to the horse were decorated with many small bells, which would ring as the sleigh moved across the snow. It was indeed a one-horse open sleigh complete with jingle bells. A vehicle that Father Christmas would have been proud of, though not in its current state.

That was how it would have been in its heyday many

years ago. Now it languished in the dark, ignored, unloved and uncared for, and slowly disappearing under piles of rotting vegetation.

Underneath all the rubbish that had been blown in, the metal supports for the wooden runners were rusty, with most of the paint having flaked off. The runners themselves were warped and cracked, the leather seating was cracked and dry, the reins were stiff with lack of care and not all the bells jingled as they should. The ultimate insult to this once beautiful mode of transport was inflicted by an owl that lived in the rafters. After a night of hunting, catching and eating small mammals the owl would regurgitate its pellets on to the seat of the sleigh. There were dozens of them piled up on the seat, looking for all the world like a huge pile of dog poo.

Now, throughout spring and summer, Lady Linton would go around the estate looking at what was stored in the various outbuildings, and she sometimes got it into her head that some of the old artefacts therein should be restored to their former glory, not for any practical reason other than it seemed to be a good idea at the time. Sometimes the subject of her interest was beyond redemption and a lot of time and effort would be wasted trying to turn a sow's ear into a silk purse. Sometimes, though, the jewel inside the rot could still be glimpsed. Such was the case of the sleigh.

One afternoon, while sitting at the Kitchen table with a cup of tea and working on some mending, I heard the call of Lady Linton summoning me from the Kitchen. I put down my needle and cotton and went to see her in the drawing room to find out what it was she wanted. She had gone out after lunch and I thought she was still out in the grounds somewhere, so it was a bit of a surprise to hear her calling me.

'Rosie, I need to speak to one of the gardeners. It doesn't matter whether it's Sam or Don. Can you find one of them and tell him to come to the front door for instructions as soon as possible?'

'Yes, Lady Linton.' I wondered what she wanted them for. Whatever it was they wouldn't be happy about it.

There were two gardeners working on the estate. Sam, the younger of the two, who was in his forties, had worked on the estate for the last fifteen years and was the more laid-back of the two. Don, the senior gardener, who was in his sixties, had grown grumpy and set in his ways over the long years of his service. Rumour had it that he was just a strapping teenager when he came to Threldale many years earlier, in the days of Lord Linton's father. Both of them lived with their families in tied cottages in the village of Hargrove, just a mile away. The day-to-day duties of the gardeners involved keeping the lawns in good condition, the drive weed-free and the Kitchen garden full of fruit and vegetables for the house.

As it was early spring I was not sure they would appreciate being disturbed. It was, after all, a busy time of the year and there was a lot of work do around the estate grounds: dead trees to fell, lawns to scarify, feed and mow, and a drive to rake. And, in the walled vegetable garden, seeds to plant, seedlings to pot on and layouts to be planned for the vegetable beds. However, I duly went round to the walled garden to seek either one of them out and disturb their day by delivering the summons from Lady Linton.

I found them both working in the greenhouses, repotting vegetable seedlings of some description from trays into individual pots. I quickly delivered Lady Linton's message and returned to my own duties in the Kitchen before either one of them could voice their concerns at being summoned away from more important jobs. Sam especially could be quite vocal if he thought he was being dragged away from what he saw as an important task to do something trivial for Lady Linton. Don tended to just have a quiet grumble to himself.

Back inside Threldale I heard the doorbell ring and decided to be nosy, so I peeked round the Kitchen passage door in time to see Lady Linton open the door and step outside to talk to the unlucky gardener. It did cross my mind that they may have tossed a coin to see who would have the unfortunate task of answering the summons. I couldn't hear what was said, so once she came back inside and had closed the front door, and on the pretext of providing Sam and Don with a treat of home-made biscuits, I went back out to the greenhouses in the walled garden to find out what was going on.

Apparently the sleigh had caught Lady Linton's attention that afternoon on one of her explorations of the outbuildings, and it was to become her latest restoration project. I have to admit I was glad that at least one of the old vehicles from the stable block was about to get the attention it deserved. Every time I peeked in the carriage bay it made me sad to see the sorry state of those carriages.

Very specific instructions had been given to Sam and Don regarding what was to be done with the sleigh. They took great pains in telling me what they had to do, and as expected they weren't happy. First of all it was to be moved from its current location in the old stable block and taken to a better location for the work to be carried out. The location chosen by Lady Linton was the modern garage at the far side of the house.

Once installed there it was to be cleared of all the detritus it had accumulated through the years of neglect. Next it was to be scrubbed from front to back and top to bottom to remove all the ingrained dirt. The leather seating, the fastenings and the reins were to be taken off the sleigh and given a good clean with leather soap and fed with a good leather polish. They were then to be repaired and refitted to the sleigh.

The metalwork was to be rubbed down to remove all signs of rust and old paint and repainted in a new colour, which Lady Linton would select as suitable for the restored sleigh. The existing old and warped wooden runners were to be removed, discarded and replaced with new ones. That just left the bells. Most of them still jingled, sort of, but some had grown completely silent with rust. Every single bell was to be cleaned in hot soapy water with a toothbrush and pipe cleaners to get out the dirt and rust from every corner and then put in my Aga to dry. The hope was that this would be enough to free up the silent bells.

This was not a job that was going to be done in a day. So, over the next few months, whenever one of the gardeners had a little time to spare, which wasn't often during a busy spring, he would disappear into the garage and do some of the work required to the sleigh. If I knew one of them was at work in the garage I would take out a mug of hot tea and a plate of home-made biscuits to give him a bit of support while he washed away the muck that came off in streams of sludgy brown muddy water. I would have to leave it outside the garage door and knock because there was just too much muck coming off the sleigh for me to go inside ... besides which, both Sam and Don had decided that once they had started the work no one, not even Lady Linton, was to see the sleigh until the work was complete. They did provide updates on how the work was progressing, though.

Slowly, over time, a clean sleigh emerged from under all the grime. Now the job of restoring the leather and the metalwork began. This took quite a bit longer to do than the initial clean-up had done. Some of the old leather was in such poor condition that it had to be either patched or discarded and replaced with new leather before it could be given a good polish.

The supports for the runners were so rusty they had to be rubbed back to remove the remaining paint and all the rust to reveal smooth metal before being painted and then waxed, to try and protect them from future problems. The old wooden runners were replaced with fresh new ash runners that had been bent, sanded, waxed and polished.

As for the bells, they took ages to bring back to their jingling prime. There were dozens of them, and they had to be worked on one at a time. Every week a tray of washed and scrubbed bells would arrive in the Kitchen to be dried off in the Aga before being returned to the gardeners. I was not allowed to take them into the garage myself. Sam and Dan asked me to leave the trays of dry bells in one of the greenhouses.

At first Lady Linton would enquire at least two or three times a week how the work was progressing, but every time she asked all the gardeners would say was that they would provide an update at the end of the week. So after a while she stopped asking, and made do with the weekly update. Then one day, several months after Lady Linton had first asked for the work to be done, there was a knock on the front door. I opened it to find both Sam and Don standing there trying to look serious, but somehow it wasn't working. They were both trying desperately not to smile.

'Rosie, can you ask Lady Linton to come to the garage, please?' said Don, furrowing his brow in an effort to smother a smile.

'Have you finished it?' I asked excitedly.

'Now that would be telling. You will have to come to the garage with Lady Linton to find out.' Sam replied, also struggling to keep a straight face.

Without another word Sam and Don turned around and headed off towards the garage whistling 'Jingle Bells'. It wasn't even Christmas! I was sure this meant that the job was finally complete and the gardeners were ready to show off their efforts.

I went into the drawing room to deliver the request to Lady Linton.

'Sam and Don would like you to come out to the garage, Lady Linton.'

'Have they finished, then?' she asked, looking at me for more information.

'I don't know, Lady Linton. They will only say they would like you to come to the garage,' I replied. I had no more information to give her. I could have told her what I was guessing but I didn't.

'Really, I haven't got time for their silly games. Are you sure they didn't say anything else?'

'Yes, I'm sure, Lady Linton.'

'I suppose I will have play along, then, but it really is too tiresome.' She stood up and headed for the front door.

Lady Linton walked round to the side of Threldale and the garage, with me tagging along behind out of sheer nosiness, to find Sam and Don standing outside with the doors firmly closed.

'We have finished the sleigh, Lady Linton,' said Don, puffing out his chest with pride.

'Well, open the doors, then!' Patience is not a word Lady Linton is familiar with and I think Sam and Don would have liked to have made more of the unveiling of the result of their months of hard work. They were obviously very pleased with the result, and it would have been a nice gesture if Lady Linton had let them have their moment.

The gardeners looked at each other, nodded, then took a door each and slowly opened them to reveal the inside of the garage. There in the centre of the floor was the sleigh, no longer an ugly duckling but now a beautiful swan. In the dim light the newly painted metalwork gleamed. The leather seating, the fittings and the reins looked supple and polished. The jingle bells sparkled and looked resplendent on the reins, and the runners looked ready to glide through the snow. It was a sight to behold.

The sleigh had been placed on a flat trolley to enable it to be moved easily. Sam and Don both grabbed the handle on the trolley and pulled the sleigh out of the gloom of the garage into the sunshine of a Yorkshire summer day. They both stepped back and allowed Lady Linton to step up to the sleigh and inspect their handiwork.

Lady Linton walked around the sleigh, closely inspecting the work that Sam and Don had put into the restoration. She stroked the painted metalwork, prodded the restored seating and shook the reins so that the bells jingled. She climbed on to the sleigh and sat down, picked up the reins, causing them to jingle again, and leant back into the seating, closing her eyes. After a minute or so she climbed out and nodded to herself.

'I knew it was a restoration we could do ourselves at

Threldale,' said Lady Linton. 'It looks very good. Now we must find somewhere better to store it so it doesn't get in the same terrible condition again, and it will need to be covered up this time to keep it clean. I will leave you both to find somewhere suitable. Just let me know where it is.' And with that pronouncement she turned around and walked back into the hall.

'Where does the "we" come into it? You and I did it, not her ladyship,' grumbled Don.

'A thank you would have been nice. That's gratitude for you.' Sam wasn't pleased either.

'Well, we had better find somewhere to store it now. I don't fancy going through that again. That was months of hard graft,' retorted Don.

'I think you have both done a wonderful job and I am sure Lady Linton appreciates your efforts really,' I said, and laughed. 'Anyway, just think of the fun you will have down in the pub in Hargrove telling everyone about how you restored the jingle bells on a one-horse open sleigh.'

The Shooting Weekend

Master Ted was fond of shooting game, a lot more than Lord Linton ever was. In fact Lord Linton no longer had any guns at Threldale and the gun cupboard was empty, as was the gamekeeper's cottage. The old gamekeeper's cottage was in danger of falling down, it was so derelict, and game had not been raised on the estate in over forty years. These days Mother Nature was allowed to grow and expand as she pleased. Where pheasants once roamed, nettles and brambles ran rampant. As the estate was pretty much a haven for nature, other animals had moved in. There were rabbits – lots of them – hares, roe deer, badgers and squirrels (sadly the grey variety, not the red).

Master Ted would often visit the shooting estates of his friends, and longed to be able to return the invitation with a shoot in the estate grounds of Threldale. Every year he would try and persuade Lord Linton to allow this to happen and every year Lord Linton would refuse. Lord Linton did not believe that his son understood estate management well enough to know what was involved in running a shooting estate.

Once upon a time the gamekeeper at Threldale would have looked after the maintenance of the woodland, the clearing of the undergrowth, the buying and the raising of the young birds, the feeding stations, the licensing and the care of the guns, the control of predators, the prevention of poaching, the engaging and the paying of the beaters, and all that before a shot was fired. The only reason I knew the little bit that I did was because my previous position had been on an estate that did a bit of private shooting within the family.

This year while Master Ted was home at Easter he was particularly persuasive, and Lord Linton finally relented and agreed – on condition that Master Ted paid for and organised every last detail of the shoot from the buying and the raising of the game to the comfort of the guests staying at Threldale, including all meals and beverages.

This was not a problem as he had the finances through various inheritances and trust funds, so the cost wasn't an issue. The issue was his lack of knowledge of organising a shooting weekend. The disruption to the daily running of the household was another matter of concern. Lord and Lady Linton were used to a peaceful existence so a Threldale of Master Ted's friends eating, drinking and shooting was not something they would relish.

Lord Linton helped out as little as possible as the plans were drawn up. I think he secretly hoped it wouldn't get beyond the planning stage. However, Master Ted was determined and a timetable was put in motion for the provision of the game birds for a shoot in late autumn. He discussed this with Sam and Don, who would have to take on the additional duties of gamekeepers, including raising the game birds and getting the estate ready for the shooting weekend. It was a huge amount of work for them to do. Besides raising the game birds they would also have to clear the nettles and the brambles, open up the woodland and police the estate against poachers and natural predators.

It would take the gardeners many months of additional work and would interfere with their other chores of looking after the huge lawns and raising the vegetables in the walled garden for the Kitchen. Lady Linton was not happy at this state of affairs and insisted that, should any conflict arise, the usual gardening activities of the gardeners would need to take precedence during the following months.

Lady Linton told Master Ted that as it was his shooting weekend she had no intention of getting involved in any of the organisation. In fact she would rather it wasn't happening at all, and couldn't understand why his father had agreed to any of it. So she (very generously) pointed him in my direction and told him to ask my advice. I can't say I was exactly happy at the prospect either. It would mean a lot of work coming my way.

Master Ted came to see me in the Kitchen with a puppy-dog look on his face to ask me what he needed to do to organise a house party for his shooting weekend. I began by asking him some basic questions.

'How many people will there be?'

'Don't know.'

'How long will they be staying?'

'Don't know.'

'What meals are to be provided?'

'Don't know.'

'What is to be on the menus?'

'Don't know.'

'How much beer, wine and spirits will be needed?'

'Don't know.'

'What rooms are to be prepared?'

'Don't know.'

'Who is to be allocated which room?'

'Don't know.'

'What about table seating plans?'

'Don't know.'

He did not have a clue about how much organising a houseful of guests staying for a few days was going to take. His eyes glazed over at the amount of work involved. I felt sorry for him, and promised I would do as much of the organising for him as I could. I could be a fool to myself at times.

There was some of the organising that Master Ted had no choice but to do himself, and this started with a weekend being chosen in mid November and agreed with Lord and Lady Linton. They promptly arranged to go and spend that weekend in London with Lord Linton's sister Tommy and her husband George in their flat in Knightsbridge, London. Mr and Mrs Kingsley-Grey had already asked them both to come down to London and stay for a few days last time they were up at Threldale for the annual trustee meeting anyway.

Next an initial list of guests was produced. They were mainly friends of Master Ted from his old school or his university in Oxford, so they would all be a good deal younger than the usual guests who came to Threldale. It was looking like there would be around twenty people, including Master Ted, for the weekend. I was now able to draw up menus and plan which rooms to prepare. Master Ted would do the seating plans and let me know which guests were to be allocated which rooms. He would also take away the menus and let me know his final decision on them within a couple of weeks.

As the year progressed invitations were sent out and acceptances received. I drew up shopping lists for all the food based on the menus that Master Ted had agreed on, after some discussion around ease of preparation, as there would only be me to do it all. Another list was produced regarding the beer, wine, spirits, mixers and fruit juices (that one seemed to be considerably larger than the one for the food). The shopping lists were then dispatched to the appropriate suppliers for fulfilment and delivery nearer the time.

November arrived, as did the deliveries to Threldale. I had a lot of preparation to do, starting with the guest rooms. Lord and Lady Linton had graciously allowed their bedroom suites to be pressed into service, as they would not be there. Master Ted was told in no uncertain terms that they must be for the use of the female guests only.

Some of the bedrooms had not been used for a long time and smelt a little musty, so were given a good dust and vacuum. Initially as many of the windows as possible were opened wide, despite the cold weather, to air the unused rooms. Once everywhere smelt a bit sweeter windows were closed, beds were made, towels put in bathrooms, radiators switched on, water flasks and glasses put on bedside tables, fires set, log baskets filled and posies of flowers put on dressing tables.

I did a quick count of beds. Lord and Lady Linton had two single beds plus the two daybeds in their dressing rooms. The Chinese bedroom had a four-poster double bed and a daybed by the window. The blue bedroom had two single beds, as did the garden bedroom. Master Ted's bedroom had a double, the rose bedroom also had a double and the lilac bedroom had two single beds. That added up to seventeen, but only if every double bed had two occupants. I was three beds short at least.

So where was I going to find three more beds? There was no way I was going to offer up my own spare bedroom. I went up to look at the six empty servants' bedrooms. One was already set up from the talk I had given to the class from Hargrove Primary School a few months before. I checked the other five bedrooms. They were dusty, smelt bad and were crammed full of junk.

I didn't have a lot of time but if I cleared out the junk from three of the rooms, gave them a good clean and put in furniture similar to what I had already put in the first bedroom, it might just work. It would mean, though, that four of Master Ted's guests would be sleeping in the attic on rickety beds with scruffy furniture and no carpets. I just hoped he would appreciate that this was the only option if he wanted to be able to house twenty people for the weekend.

Every spare minute I had over the next week or so I spent in the old servants' bedrooms, and by the time I was finished I had basic sleeping accommodation for four more guests. It would be down to Master Ted to decide who would get the short straw and finish up in a servant's room rather than a guest room.

Back down in the Kitchen a lot of baking was done. I made biscuits, both sweet and savoury, cakes and bread. When drawing up the menus I had taken the opportunity of putting lots of things on them that could be prepared and cooked ahead of the weekend then frozen. So the freezers began to fill with a variety of dishes for snacking, and for the informal lunches and the formal suppers. I was lucky that there were two large chest freezers, one in the Kitchen and one in the garden room. There had been nowhere else to put the second freezer when it had arrived a couple of years earlier.

On the Friday morning of the shooting weekend Lord and Lady Linton left for London after a leisurely breakfast, leaving me to look after Threldale and Master Ted's guests. I was under strict instructions from Lady Linton not to allow Master Ted to make too much mess, make too much noise, get too drunk or generally abuse the trust they were putting in him. How I was supposed to do all that was a mystery to me. He was over twenty-one, he would be the owner of Threldale one day, and I was merely employed to cook and clean. If he chose to do so he could tell to keep my nose out. This was his shooting weekend, after all.

By late afternoon the guests began to arrive and were shown up to their rooms. There was to be an informal supper on the first evening in the Dining Room, and so the guests did not need to dress up for the occasion. I would serve the first course and then put the main course in chafing dishes on the sideboard for them to serve themselves. Dessert would also be left on the sideboard on trays in individual glass bowls. The theory was that I would get an early night on the Friday, as on Saturday I would be up very late catering for the formal supper.

It all seemed to go very well and I was able to retire at 10 p.m. I have no idea what time Master Ted and his guests retired, but the Dining Room was an absolute pigsty the next morning when I entered it at 7.30 a.m. There were dirty dishes all over the dining table, the sideboard, the window ledges, the floor – in fact, over every level surface. There was food trampled into the carpet and cigarette ends stubbed out in various dinner plates and dessert dishes. Empty bottles lay everywhere, and judging by the number of them I was not sure the supplies of drink would last the weekend.

While I could have got upset at the mess, that would not have cleared it up, or got breakfast ready by 10 a.m., so I rolled up my sleeves and got on with the job.

I was so busy the next couple of hours just whizzed by, clearing and washing dishes, throwing out waste food and empty bottles, wiping down furniture and cleaning carpets. By 9.30 a.m. I was ready to get breakfast cooked and set up the Dining Room for 10 a.m. It would be a bit of a push but I knew I could just about do it. The plan was to have everyone up, dressed, fed and ready for a day's shooting by 11 a.m. I just had to make sure the bacon, sausages, mushrooms, tomatoes, eggs, toast, coffee and orange juice were ready for everyone when they came down to the Dining Room for breakfast.

I needn't have worried about getting everything done by 10 a.m. as it was 11.30 a.m. before anyone appeared and that was Master Ted, looking very tired and hung-over.

'We had great fun last night playing a few drinking games. We didn't get to bed until 5.30 a.m. We may need to get in more beer and wine – oh, and cigarettes. Can you organise that?'

'Certainly, Master Ted.' No point spoiling his weekend by complaining.

'Good. I have decided to move the shoot back to 12 p.m. as I think most people are sleeping late. We will have breakfast before we leave.'

'It is all ready, Master Ted.' I would have liked to have added that it had been ready since 10 a.m. but

I didn't.

Slowly, over the next half hour, the rest of the guests appeared, looking very bleary-eyed, hung-over and some still the worse for drink. Some of these people would be using guns within the next hour or so. As far as I knew there would only be five guns, but looking at them trying to eat breakfast and stay awake at the same time worried me.

Sam had been asked to work that day and keep a close eye on the guns. He had come in for his own breakfast hours ago and was waiting to get going in the Kitchen. Once most of the guests were down I went back to the Kitchen to apprise him of the state of his charges. While not very happy at the prospect I knew Sam was made of stern stuff and would keep them in line.

As it was they did not leave Threldale until 12.30 p.m. The morning shoot had changed into an afternoon shoot. They were all wrapped up against the cold, topped off with wellingtons and waterproofs, and they did not expect to be back until the light failed. Once again I set to turning around the Dining Room ready for the formal supper that evening. I was done by 2 p.m., so I then set about cleaning up the drawing room and the billiard room followed by valeting the bedrooms, filling log baskets, cleaning the bathrooms and emptying the rubbish bins.

I was barely finished when Master Ted and the guests arrived back at 4.15 p.m. with the results of the afternoon's shoot – just a single brace of pheasants. I wasn't surprised at the low game count, judging by the way they had looked when they set out.

Now they were back they had all gone from looking bleary-eyed and hung-over to looking cold and hungry. I had pots of hot chocolate and coffee and plates of biscuits and cake ready for them to tuck into while I went back to sorting out the courses for the formal supper. Sam was waiting for me in the Kitchen looking tired and fed up, so I told to get off home and that I could manage from this point on.

The hot drinks and snacks went down well, and by 6 p.m. everyone had retired to their rooms to bathe and change ready for pre-supper drinks at 7.30 p.m. The men were to wear dinner suits and the ladies evening gowns. They would go into the Dining Room for supper at 8 p.m. and I would serve the first course at 8.15 p.m. I won't go into the detail of the supper other than to say that following my serving of the main course and the dessert course, I took in the final fruit and cheeseboard in at 11 p.m. After that I tidied up the Kitchen ready for the morning and got to my bed at 12.30 a.m., utterly exhausted, and promptly fell fast asleep.

I would like to be able to say that the Dining Room wasn't as bad the next morning, but it was. I think it was a bigger mess than the night before, but the Dining Room wasn't the worst mess that I faced. I opened the front door and on the doorstep was a dead roe deer, a dead fox and two dead rabbits. It didn't stop there. The buggy used to drive around the estate grounds was on its side on the front lawn, surrounded by deep tyre marks gouged into the grass.

I quickly shut the door. This was one mess that was beyond me. Lord and Lady Linton would not be happy when they returned on the Monday. I could only do my best inside Threldale itself. Master Ted would have to sort out the results of the massacre outside.

When Master Ted finally came down to breakfast he looked not only hung-over but worried as well.

'I have an awful feeling we went out shooting last night after supper.'

'Yes, Master Ted, you did.'

'Did we shoot anything?'

'Yes, you did.'

'Where have we left whatever we shot?'

'On the front doorstep.'

'What did we shoot?'

'One roe deer, one fox and two rabbits.'

'How did we get around?'

'The estate buggy.'

'Where is it now?'

'On the front lawn on its side.'

'I had better go and take a look.'

He turned around and left the Dining Room. I heard the front door open and waited. After a minute or so I heard the door close and Master Ted returning.

'Will you be able to clean all that up outside?'

'No, Master Ted. I have far too much to do already inside the house.'

'You must help me. I will be in so much trouble with Mama.'

'I really do have too much to do, Master Ted.'

'Well, if you won't help me, I will have to do it myself, then.' He sounded like a spoilt child. If he was trying to make me feel guilty about not helping him sort out the mess, he failed. On top of that I wasn't hopeful that Master Ted had any idea about how to sort out the mess outside the front door. But it wasn't my problem.

Everyone else came down in ones and twos over the next few hours, and as a result Sunday was a much quieter day. The guests had a long, leisurely brunch and by mid afternoon some of them began packing up to leave. I did provide a simple Sunday roast at 6 p.m. for those few guests leaving later in the evening. By 9 p.m. the last of the guests had gone and there was only Master Ted and me left. Throughout the day I had done the best I could, in between looking after the guests, to get on top of the cleaning up, but inside Threldale was not looking its best. I didn't dare look outside. It was up to Master Ted to work that problem out.

Needless to say, when Lord and Lady Linton returned on Monday afternoon they were furious at the disrespect that had been shown to the grounds of Threldale Hall. As far as inside the hall was concerned I had managed to get most of the mess cleared up in the reception rooms downstairs during Monday morning. I had also managed to get Lord and Lady Linton's bedroom suites returned to their former state by removing rubbish, putting clean bedding on the beds and fresh towels in the bathrooms, and by dusting, wiping and vacuuming. The other guest bedrooms were untouched, awaiting my attention. They would have to be cleaned in between my other chores over the next few weeks. It would be a long time before I was happy that all vestiges of the weekend had been removed.

As for the fallout, Master Ted was told by Lord Linton to find someone to fix the front lawns and pay for it out of his own pocket. The gardeners had been told not to touch it. Lady Linton was furious that so much mess had been made in so many rooms and that it was going to take me weeks to get Threldale back to its former glory. Months later I was still finding little pockets that I had missed.

Master Ted was not allowed to have another shooting weekend at Threldale. In fact, I overheard Lord Linton say he would be in his grave before he would give Master Ted the run of Threldale again.

Home for Christmas

It was early December and I was starting to think about preparations for Christmas. This wasn't an easy task as I had no idea what Lord and Lady Linton's plans were, and I am not sure even they knew at that point.

As I sat in the Kitchen I daydreamed about them going away to stay with friends, leaving me to have a quiet and relaxing holiday – no meals to cook, no rooms to clean, and getting up late and going to bed early. Of course, that was never going to happen. Lord Linton hated going away for Christmas or New Year. Still, I would like to know how busy I was going to be and what time I would get off to celebrate my own Christmas.

The weather had turned frosty but it was doubtful that it would snow, so there would probably be no white Christmas. I don't think there had been a white Christmas in all my ten years at Threldale. The snow tended to arrive in our little dale in January or February, or if we were really unlucky in March. I knew at least one white Easter during my time there.

That morning, though, it had just been very cold. Threldale looked very pretty when the lawns glistened with frost, and the ground in the woodlands was hard enough to walk on without getting muddy. I wasn't that bothered about snow, but I would have liked to have known when I would have time off over the Christmas festivities.

Mid morning I took a tray of coffee and biscuits up to the drawing room, wondering how to broach the subject with Lady Linton. However, I need not have worried.

'Thank you, Rosie. Before you go I have been discussing what we are doing over Christmas with His Lordship. Teddy isn't coming home this year. He is talking of spending Christmas at Oxford with his friends, so we think it will be just the two of us this year. That being the case, and providing you finish all the required preparations, I don't think we will need you on Christmas Day and Boxing Day. You can finish at the end of Christmas Eve and we won't need to see you again until the twenty-seventh. Are you happy with those arrangements?'

'Yes, Lady Linton.' I couldn't believe my luck. Two whole days off. I almost skipped back down to the Kitchen. Preparing meals for two people for two days would be easy-peasy. Teddy was the Honourable Edward Hadyn Bertram Linton, the only son and heir of Lord and Lady Linton, but to me he was Master Ted. The fact that he was not coming home was a bonus, as his presence usually gave me lots of extra work to do. It was going to be a great Christmas.

What was I thinking? Things are never that straightforward. Later that same week Lady Linton had some information for me regarding changes to the Christmas arrangements we had agreed only a few days earlier.

'Good news, Rosie! Teddy has changed his mind. None of his friends are staying on in Oxford over Christmas, so he is coming home to spend it with us. We are going to need you after all. We will make up your time off in the new year. You won't have had time to organise anything yet for those two days off, would you? Good. I knew you would be as pleased as I am.' I was so disappointed. My daydream lay shattered in tiny pieces at my feet.

'Wonderful news, Lady Linton,' I said, trying to sound as pleased as she thought I was.

I trudged back to the Kitchen, my hopes of a peaceful Christmas gone for this year. At least it would only be the three of them. It could still be a fairly quiet Christmas if I got well prepared beforehand. It was only more mouth to feed, after all. It wasn't as if there was going to be a houseful of people.

The next day Mr and Mrs George Kingsley-Grey, Lord Linton's brother-in-law and younger sister Tommy, came for lunch on their way back from a shooting weekend in Scotland. They had a large flat in Knightsbridge in London, so stopping off at Threldale was a welcome break on the journey home. Their lives revolved around their social calendar: tennis, travel and garden parties in the summer, and skiing holidays, the theatre, shooting and dinner parties throughout the winter. Lord and Lady Linton found the social whirl of London much too exhausting when they went down to stay in Knightsbridge and were always glad to get back to the peace of Threldale.

While serving lunch I was able to overhear Mrs Tommy Kingsley-Grey bemoaning to Lord Linton the lack of any Christmas arrangements she had in place for her and her husband, George.

'Charles, what am I to do with myself?' sighed Mrs Kingsley-Grey, addressing him directly. 'There is not enough snow for us to spend Christmas in Italy skiing on the slopes, which is what we had planned. It is too late to try and get anything booked in Switzerland or Austria. Every decent hotel in London is booked solid from Christmas Eve through to Boxing Day and all our friends have made plans already. And, unfortunately, as we expected to be out of the country, they don't include us.

'How can I be expected to stay at home in our flat and organise Christmas for George and myself? I wouldn't know where to begin. I mean, how does one decorate a tree or cook Christmas lunch? Every show in town is sold out, so how on earth do I keep George entertained for two whole days? I am completely out of ideas.'

Lord Linton beamed at his sister.

'Goodness me, Tommy! The answer is right in front of you. Isn't it, dear?' he continued, looking at Lady Linton.

'Yes, you must come here. We have oodles of room. Rosie has no plans, so she is working right through this year and can easily cope with a couple of extra guests. Can't you, Rosie?' she said, looking at me expectantly.

'Yes, Lady Linton, of course I can.' I managed to smile though inside I was groaning at the increasing amount of work. As for having no plans, Lady Linton was making me sound like Billy No-Mates. In a few days Christmas had gone from a bit of forward planning and preparation with Christmas Day and Boxing Day off to working both days and catering Christmas for five people over three days. I hoped and prayed that there would be no more additions but prepared myself for the worst, as the worst is usually what happened at Threldale where I was concerned.

It was with no great surprise that the very next day I had another conversation regarding Christmas with Lady Linton while I was clearing away breakfast.

'It looks like we are in for a jolly Christmas this year after all, Rosie. Dottie Pettigrew is coming for Christmas with her husband, Nigel.'

'Yes, Lady Linton.' I looked at her for clarification. I had no idea who she was talking about.

'Mrs Dorothea Pettigrew is an old friend. We go back years. Dottie and Nigel live in the Home Counties on a lovely shooting estate with stunning views across open countryside. We went to stay with them for a week during the summer a couple of years ago and had a lovely time. They have builders in doing repair work on a leaking roof and have asked if they can come to stay for a few days to get away from the noise and dust. I have told them they must come for Christmas.'

'Yes, Lady Linton.' The numbers were just going up

and up.

'There is more. Dowager Lady Linton, His Lordship's mother, is also coming for a few days. We are going to be quite a houseful. Isn't it exciting?' Lady Linton was getting quite giddy at having so many guests staying over Christmas, which is more than I was.

'Yes, Lady Linton. It's going to be quite a family Christmas.' I did my best to sound equally excited.

So we now had eight for Christmas. This would need some serious forward planning and preparation. The next couple of weeks were a dizzying round of cleaning and setting up rooms, planning menus, writing shopping lists and arranging supermarket deliveries. Then there was the cooking, and a Christmas cake, Christmas puddings, mince pies, shortbread, candied fruits and chocolate truffles to make as well.

By the twenty-third of December I had everything in the Kitchen ready and I was in a position to begin decorating the Entrance Hall, the drawing room and the Dining Room ready for the festivities. I began by sorting out the holly and ivy that the gardeners had cut from trees in the grounds and left in the garden room for me. Lady Linton preferred natural decorations.

I decorated the mantels over the fireplaces, the mirrors, the paintings and over the door frames with lots of holly, glass baubles and red ribbon. Next I wound the ivy around the banister and the newel posts on the staircase and tied them in place with more red ribbon. With the holly, ivy and red ribbon that was left I did my best to make a wreath for the front door using some wire begged from Sam to support the greenery. It looked quite good, so I got Sam to hang it on the front door for me.

A bare tree stood in the Entrance Hall. This had been sourced by Don from a supplier in the next dale who specialised in growing Christmas trees, so this was next for my Christmas ministrations. Lady Linton did not approve of lights on the tree so I stuck with glass baubles, ribbon, cinnamon sticks and slices of oranges and lemons that I had dried in the Aga for this purpose. By the end of the day both Threldale Hall and I were ready to receive Lord and Lady Linton's Christmas guests. I was a little tired with all the preparations, but once the guests arrived then my work would really begin in earnest.

On the following day, Christmas Eve, the first guest to arrive was the Dowager Lady Linton. Lord Linton had gone to pick her up from her home, a dower house provided for her by the estate in York, straight after he had finished his breakfast. When they returned later that morning she sailed into the hall first, followed by Lord Linton bearing two suitcases.

'Put the bags down, Charles. You should have left them in the car for Rosie to bring in. Speaking of which, Rosie, take my bags up to my room.' She looked rather pointedly at me.

'Yes, Lady Linton. I'll put them in the blue bedroom, as usual,' I said as I acknowledged her request. This bedroom was the coldest in the house but for some reason it was the one that the Dowager Lady Linton preferred, probably for its views across the front lawns and down the dale towards Hargrove village.

This was going to be a difficult few days with two Lady Lintons in residence, both with strong personalities.

'I'll take tea in the drawing room with Lady Linton when you've done that, Rosie.'

'Yes, Lady Linton. I have taken the liberty of putting a tea tray in the drawing room already.'

'Now, Charles, where is Arabella?' she said, turning to Lord Linton.

'She is in the drawing room awaiting your arrival, Mama.'

With that they both disappeared into the drawing room to have tea with Lady Linton, leaving me alone in the hall to take the dowager's cases up to her room. I went to pick them both up to take upstairs and nearly fell over with the weight. What did she have in them? In the end I had to take them up to her bedroom one at a time and then go and get myself a cup of tea in the Kitchen to recover.

Next to arrive, just after midday, were Mr and Mrs Pettigrew, who were shown through to the garden bedroom at the back of the house on the ground floor by yours truly. I hope they didn't mind that it was a twin room. Thankfully Mr Pettigrew insisted on carrying their bags. I left them in their room to settle in while I returned to preparing lunch.

Lunch was served at 1 p.m. in the Dining Room, which I had set up for four prior to the arrival of the Pettigrews. I had prepared a selection of cold dishes earlier that morning: pasta salad, coronation chicken, mixed salad, a tomato salsa and fresh baked bread rolls. This meant I could be more relaxed about numbers and just needed to set two more places for the new arrivals.

Lady Linton and Mrs Pettigrew chatted away throughout lunch, catching up on gossip. Mr Pettigrew, Lord Linton and his mother discussed gardening, a burning interest of the dowager's but not of Lord Linton's, however, he did his best to appear interested in the subject. Mr Pettigrew, it appeared, did have a great interest in gardening, something that could be a challenge on a shooting estate where the raising of game birds tended to take priority over roses and cabbages. There was some idle talk of going out to look at the vegetables in the walled garden after lunch. Sam and Don would love that. They would be keen to get away to their own families for Christmas.

It was late afternoon before the final arrivals made their appearance. The doorbell rang and when I opened it Mr and Mrs Kingsley-Grey bustled in with their arms full of boxes and bags, which they immediately deposited in a pile on the floor of the Entrance Hall. It would appear that they had been doing some last-minute shopping in Leeds after they had got off the London train. The last leg of their journey had been by taxi, which must have been so full there could hardly have been room for the Kingsley-Greys. The taxi driver came in behind them with two suitcases, which he put down next to the existing pile of baggage, said his goodbyes, and, before you knew it, was away down the drive to return to Leeds.

The Kingsley-Greys were greeted by a beaming Lady Linton. Lord Linton had retired to the Library after lunch to finish reading the morning paper and the dowager had gone to her room for a nap. Since hitting her nineties she seemed to tire easily. The Pettigrews had retreated to their room to finish unpacking their bags and settle in.

'We are so looking forward to a family Christmas! I am quite beside myself with excitement,' Mrs Kingsley-Grey said, beaming. 'Who else is here?'

'Hello, Tommy! Come in, come in. Mama is here. She arrived before lunch, and she's gone for a nap. She is a little tired after the drive over from York. Charles picked her up this morning. Now do you remember my old chum Dottie Fairfax? She married Nigel Pettigrew. Well, she is here with her husband. Teddy is due home from Oxford, of course, so he should be here soon.' She paused and then continued,

'Rosie, take the bags up to their room, and when you come back down we will have coffee in the drawing room. We'll have some Scottish shortbread with our coffee.'

'Yes, Lady Linton.'

They were staying in the rather grand Chinese bedroom. It took me three trips up and down the stairs to get all the parcels, bags and suitcases up there. At least I didn't have to unpack any of it. It was going to be a long and very busy Christmas.

Supper on Christmas Eve was for seven, as there was

no sign of Master Ted. It was a simple beef casserole with mixed roasted vegetables, followed by hot mince pies with a brandy cream. Lady Linton had taken a telephone message from Master Ted earlier in the evening to say he would be dining out with friends in Oxford and then driving up to Threldale later in the evening. It would now be very late before he would arrive, and the rest of the household would probably already be asleep by then.

I was able to retire to my flat by 10 p.m. I had a hot bath, made a mug of cocoa and put my feet up for a short while before going to bed. At least I wouldn't have to wait up for Master Ted. He had his own key and, while the rest of the house would be locked and secure, the front door would not be barred. I didn't hear him come in, but he was there the next morning at breakfast.

I don't remember feeling very Christmassy over the next two days, I was so busy. Christmas Day began with a light breakfast before everyone, except me, the very busy housekeeper, left for the morning service at St Luke's in Hargrove village.

While they were gone I cleared away breakfast and valeted all the occupied bedrooms. On their return at midday drinks were served, along with sandwiches, shortbread and hot mince pies, after which they played parlour games. At three o'clock everyone sat down to listen to the Queen's speech, and then presents were exchanged and opened. A traditional Christmas dinner with all the trimmings was served at 7 p.m. and went on until 10 p.m. with me cooking, serving and clearing each of the courses. I collapsed, exhausted, into my bed at half past midnight. I hadn't cleared the Dining Room of the remains of the Christmas dinner, nor had I left the Kitchen as clean and tidy as I usually would. It would have to wait until morning.

Boxing Day was a little bit easier. I was up by 7 a.m. and cleaning the Kitchen and Dining Room ready for breakfast. By 8.30 a.m. the Dining Room was set up ready for a breakfast of bacon, sausage, mushrooms, tomatoes, eggs and toast. There were a couple of large jugs of freshly squeezed orange juice and I would take in tea and coffee once people began to appear. In the meantime I was able to clean the drawing room and the Entrance Hall before returning to the Kitchen for a well-earned cup of tea.

Lord Linton, Mr Nigel Pettigrew, Mr George Kingsley-Grey and Master Ted were all down by 9 a.m. for an early breakfast before leaving to go shooting on another estate only an hour's drive away. The ladies had a later breakfast and joined the men later on for lunch. At least that was one meal I was spared having to prepare. Once they had all gone I valeted the rooms, cleaned up the Dining Room again, by one thirty I was done until they all returned.

After a few hours my peace was shattered when everyone returned at five thirty, all complaining of being ravenously hungry. I prepared a couple of plates of turkey salad sandwiches and a cheeseboard with some grapes and put them in the drawing room. That way I could set up the Dining Room for supper later that evening.

Supper started with figs baked with goat's cheese followed by salmon en croute with duchesse potatoes and two vegetables, and finished with a chocolate mousse. It was served at eight with all courses cooked, served and cleared by me, and again it was half past midnight before I crept into my bed.

The morning of the twenty-seventh dawned and it was a glorious morning, from my perspective anyway. Both the Pettigrews and the Kingsley-Greys would be leaving today. Breakfast was very late – it was 11.30 a.m. by the time everyone was down – and drifted on to towards lunchtime. I had perhaps gone a bit overboard with porridge, bacon, sausages, mushrooms, tomatoes, scrambled eggs, kippers, toast, croissants, fruit, juices, tea and coffee.

'Don't worry about lunch today, Rosie,' mumbled Lady Linton from behind a morning paper she was perusing.

'No, Lady Linton.' Another plus. The day was getting better all the time.

'We don't want any fuss today. We will just carry on grazing on the contents of the chafing dishes.'

'Yes, Lady Linton.'

She wasn't kidding. It was 2 p.m. by the time the Dining Room was vacated and I was able to clear away breakfast and every empty chafing dish.

By 3 p.m. both the Pettigrews and the Kingsley-Greys had packed their bags, brought them downstairs and put them in their respective cars and were ready to go. Lord and Lady Linton stood by the open front door to see them off.

'We had a lovely time, thank you, dear.' Mrs Pettigrew gave Lady Linton a peck on each cheek. Mr Pettigrew made do with a handshake and a gruff,

'Yes, thank you, most enjoyable.'

'Now go and put your feet up. You've worked so hard this Christmas. I don't know how you managed to produce such a fantastic feast and such wonderful entertainment. You've earned a rest after looking after us so well over the last few days. This is one Christmas I will remember for a long time,' she continued.

'I don't know how we would have got through Christmas without you, Arabella,' said Mrs Kingsley-Grey. 'You have been an absolute poppet. I agree with Dottie here. You go and put your feet up once we have gone. I don't know where you got your energy from over the last few days. I certainly couldn't do it.'

With that they piled into their respective cars and drove down the drive away from Threldale.

'That was one of the best Christmases we have had at Threldale don't you think?' said Lady Linton, looking at me for confirmation.

'It was very much an old-fashioned family Christmas, Lady Linton,' I replied diplomatically.

Master Ted and the Dowager Lady Linton stayed on another day, but at least the workload had lessened considerably by then. I was so looking forward to getting back those days off in the new year after I had worked so hard. Maybe I would get next Christmas off.

The Dowager's Funeral

During the last week of February Lord Linton received some sad news. His mother, the Dowager Lady Linton, had passed away in her ninety-fourth year. It would appear she caught a chill while out in her garden hacking back an overgrown corner on a particularly frosty day. She had been a very keen gardener and would quite happily talk for hours on the subject.

She had taken to her bed when the chill had become a heavy cold and, despite the tender ministrations of her own housekeeper and the regular attendance of the doctor, she departed this mortal life several days later. She had seemed so hale and hearty when she had come to stay for Christmas that it was difficult for Lord Linton to comprehend. There had been no sign of any frailty. In fact she had been her usual formidable self.

On the specific instructions of the Dowager Lady Linton herself, her remains were to come home to Threldale Hall to rest in state in the Entrance Hall for a few days once the initial formalities had been completed. This was where she had lived for many years with her husband, the eighth Earl Linton, before he had passed away and the current Lord Linton became the ninth earl. After that period in state she would leave for burial in the family plot in the churchyard of St Luke's in Hargrove village.

The dowager had loved Threldale Hall and the dale it sat in, and at the time she had been reluctant to leave it when her son inherited the title and estate. She was the person responsible for a lot of the planting of the trees and shrubs on the estate during the time of her tenure many years ago. When she had finally left Threldale it was to move to a dower house, which had been provided for her by Lord Linton. She had chosen the property in York for its extensive gardens, and it was to this house that she had retired to on giving up Threldale. It was in the garden of this house where she had caught the fatal chill.

The passing of a close member of the Linton family was a whole new experience for me, and I had no idea what to expect or what the protocol was. There had been a steady stream of events and happenings at Threldale over the years but to date there hadn't been a family funeral, and certainly not the funeral of a member of the aristocracy. What would I be expected to do, if anything? How grand was the funeral going to be? Who would attend the service?

I need not have worried. The late dowager had left detailed written instructions behind. She was as organised in death as she had been in life. She was leaving nothing to chance. The local family firm of undertakers who had dealt with the Linton family for generations held a document containing all the late dowager's wishes. Lord Linton also held a copy, and between them they would see them carried out.

The undertakers came to Threldale to discuss the document left by the dowager with Lord Linton, and it was agreed to carry out her instructions as stated and unchanged in any way. The first instruction listed in the document concerned the coffin. Before it could be readied to receive the remains of the late dowager, Lord Linton was to arrange with the local blacksmith to have the handles and other fittings cast from parts of an old iron cannon, in line with a similar thing having being done for her late husband's coffin. The same patterns were to be used. Once the fittings and handles had been cast and attached to the coffin, the dowager was to be laid to rest inside. The coffin would then be secured and brought to Threldale to lie in state until the funeral.

This cannon dated back several hundred years, and had been found on the estate by Lord Linton's father when having restoration work carried out on the old folly. Nobody knew where it had come from but the late Lord Linton had had it cleaned up, and it sat outside the front door for the remainder of his lifetime. On his death it was moved to the premises of the local blacksmith for the work to be carried out. The cannon was still stored there after being used to cast the fittings for the late Lord Linton's coffin.

On the day of the funeral the coffin would be placed on a carriage pulled by a single black horse. This would then set off at the head of the funeral cortège with the mourners, who were not going directly to the church, following on foot. A stop would be made at the gates of the estate for the mourners walking behind the carriage to be supplied with a warming hot toddy, before continuing on to the church in Hargrove. The dowager even provided details of the contents of the hot toddy, which was to be made of one part whisky to two parts hot water with a squeeze of lemon and a drizzle of honey.

Once at the church the service would take place in accordance with the dowager's predefined service order. She had left details of the readings and the hymns for the vicar to follow. She instructed Lord Linton to write and deliver the elegy, listing what he could and could not include in it. The coffin would then leave the church followed by the cortège and would move into the church grounds for the interment to take place in the family plot, where the dowager would join her late husband, the eighth earl. The carriage, cortège and mourners would then return to Threldale, still on foot, for refreshments to be served in the ground-floor reception rooms.

That in essence was the plan. If only it went off that smoothly!

Lord Linton passed on the late dowager's request to the local blacksmith, the same man who had cast all the fittings for his father's coffin. The blacksmith set to work and, using the cannon and the same patterns, he carried out the request in accordance with the dowager's wishes and delivered the completed iron fittings to Threldale just a couple of days later.

Lord Linton took charge of them, promising he would get in touch with the undertakers to have them picked up and then fitted to the coffin. In the meantime he put them away in a safe place of his choosing. The undertakers called to pick them up later that same day and somehow, in that short intervening period, Lord Linton had forgotten where he had put them. He insisted they were not lost, merely stored safely somewhere. He just couldn't remember where.

There followed a lot of heated discussion between Lord and Lady Linton about where the safe place was and how could Lord Linton be so careless as to forget the location. Rooms were searched and cupboards rummaged in, some several times. I was asked if I had seen them or moved them. I hadn't. I was also asked to help with the search, not that I had any more idea than Lady Linton where Lord Linton had put them.

Just when it seemed that either a new set would have to be cast or a more off-the-shelf solution adopted, which would have been very much against the dowager's wishes, Lord Linton remembered where he had put them. For some reason he had stored them in the old gun cupboard, now empty of any guns, as it had a lock on it and they would be safe in there as only he had a key to that cupboard. He went and got the key to the gun cupboard, unlocked it, and retrieved the package containing the fittings for the coffin.

The undertakers took the (now safely recovered) fittings back to the funeral parlour, where they used them to complete the construction of the coffin. Once

191

this was done the remains of the dowager were carefully and respectfully placed inside and the lid secured. The next day they returned to the hall with the dowager, and a bier was set up in the Entrance Hall to put the coffin on.

A single candle in a silver candlestick on a tall wooden stand was placed at each of the four corners. The gardeners had made up the four stands at short notice, and they actually looked quite good. They had taken the trouble to not only build the stands but also to sand them smooth and give them a coat of varnish. The finished stands looked as if they were part and parcel of the furnishings at Threldale and not something quickly put together with whatever Sam and Don had to hand.

This was to be the dowager's resting place for the next three days prior to the funeral. One of my more unusual duties during this time was to light the candles each morning, replacing them as they burnt down and to put them out each night. Some people might think this to be quite a morbid task but for some strange reason I didn't. Instead I found myself saying 'Good morning' and 'Goodnight' to the late dowager on each of the three days. I thought I would have been at least slightly spooked at having a body in the house but I wasn't. Instead it seemed to be the right way to say goodbye to a grand old lady. I even found myself talking to her if I happened to be cleaning in the Entrance Hall, and I'm sure she didn't mind.

The day of the funeral was cold and bright, the sun shone out of a clear blue sky, the air was crisp and the ground hard with frost. It was going to be a cold walk to the church but at least it wasn't raining or blowing a gale. The service was at midday so Lord and Lady Linton were both up by 10 a.m. ready for breakfast in the Dining Room. Both were more subdued than they normally would be and took their breakfast in relative silence, in keeping with the sombre occasion.

Lady Linton looked suitably attired in a black jersey dress with a single rope of pearls around her neck. She had laid out a black woollen coat, a cream handbag and cream hat with a black band on her bed ready to put on later in the day. Lord Linton wore a dark suit, a white shirt and a black tie, which he would top off with a black woollen coat for the walk. He would not be wearing a hat. He loathed hats. Master Ted was driving up from Oxford and was expected to arrive by 11 a.m.

I would not be attending the funeral. Lady Linton decided I would be of much more use if I stayed behind. I was to get Threldale ready for the returning mourners by lighting fires, putting on lights, arranging the seating and setting up the bathrooms attached to a couple of the guest rooms for use as facilities for the mourners. Estimates of numbers coming back ranged between 150 and 200, a wide range but not an issue, unless they all needed access to the bathrooms at the same time. Hopefully that was not going to happen.

I did not have to do any of the catering, not even

the hot toddy. Caterers were on hand to provide refreshments. They were scheduled to arrive at 11 a.m. and start preparing things in the Kitchen. All I had to do was settle them in and make sure they had everything they needed. The caterers would also be making up the hot toddy according to the dowager's instructions. Two waitresses would take it, ahead of the funeral cortège (in several insulated flasks, with fifty small tot glasses), to the gates to give to the mourners as they passed on their way out of the estate. By that point they would all be feeling the cold, and the hot toddy would be a welcome warmer.

The funeral cortège was scheduled to set off from Threldale at 11.20 a.m. It would take around thirty minutes to walk at a respectably slow pace to the church, around a mile away, with an additional ten minutes for the stop at the gates to the estate to drink the hot toddy. By 11.15 a.m. there were about sixty or seventy people standing around on the driveway making small talk and sharing memories of the late dowager. Most of the other mourners were going directly to the church in Hargrove.

At the appropriate time a line of bearers was formed and the coffin was lifted from the bier in the Entrance Hall. It was then taken out of the front door and placed on a slightly raised platform on the carriage, which had been covered with a dark green woollen blanket, and surrounded by family flowers. The procession set off at exactly 11.20 a.m. The carriage was drawn by the single black horse, and was followed by the family and then the mourners who wished to walk behind the coffin. I watched from the doorway until the last of the mourners fell in line at the back of the procession and moved off down the driveway. Then I went inside to ready the house for their return.

The service and the interment would take about an hour and it would be another half hour after that before the mourners began to arrive back at Threldale at an estimated 1.30 p.m., so I had time for a quick cup of tea before making sure all the tasks allocated to me were carried out in plenty of time. The caterers needed no help from me. The food was all finger food with plates and napkins supplied by them, and the drink was a selection of hot and cold beverages, alcoholic and non-alcoholic. I didn't even have to provide cups, saucers or glasses.

The two waitresses had left Threldale at 11.15 a.m. in the caterers' van ahead of the cortège so they would not get in the way of the mourners walking towards the gates of the estate. By all accounts the hot toddy went down well, turning the breath of the mourners to steam in the cold air and helping to make the walk a little easier. When the waitresses returned at 11.50 a.m. all the flasks were empty and the tot glasses sticky with the residue of the hot toddy.

At an appropriate time a car was sent to the church to bring back Lord and Lady Linton separately from the mourners. They were not expected to have to walk back from the church to Threldale. They also wished to be in a position to welcome the mourners to Threldale and accept condolences in a relaxed atmosphere.

Back at the church, the now empty horse-drawn carriage, returned to Threldale through the estate, followed by all the mourners. The plan was that by the time they arrived back at Threldale, after Lord and Lady Linton, they would be cold and hungry, seeking refreshment and, more importantly, warmth. The returning cortège was now considerably bigger than when it had set out from the house, as the mourners who had arrived at the church by car had left their vehicles in the village. There was no hot toddy provided on the walk back to keep out the cold.

But by the time the mourners did begin to arrive Lord and Lady Linton were surprised to find that most of them were trying to stifle the giggles. Not very respectful behaviour on such a sad occasion. After gently quizzing some of mourners the reason became clear. Apparently, as the horse pulled the carriage through the gates on to the estate, it went over a bump in the road and one of the wheels came off and rolled away down the road.

One of the undertakers had to run after it while the other members of the cortège had rushed to hold up the carriage and stop anything else falling off − not that there was anything else to fall off by then. The wheel was duly reattached to the carriage and the journey back to Threldale completed without any further mishap, though a close watch was kept on the offending axle and wheel. It was not lost on anyone that had this happened on the walk to the church it would have been disastrous.

I waited at the front door to guide those arriving and to inform them where they could get warm in front of an open fire, obtain refreshments after the cold walk back from the church, visit the bathroom or deposit their coats. There was a lot of nose blowing and hand rubbing as everyone tried to get warm again and restore some circulation to their cold extremities. The fires were a welcome way of defrosting their hands and feet.

The partaking of refreshments turned out to be a much more cheerful affair than one would have expected. The late Dowager Lady Linton would have appreciated the humour of the wheel falling off, though I am not sure that Lord and Lady Linton did. They moved among the mourners recalling memories of the dowager and her husband in times past. It had been many years since the dowager had lived at Threldale but she was still fondly remembered as a force to be reckoned with in the area.

There seemed to be copious amounts of cold alcoholic beverages being consumed by, I assumed to be, the non-drivers and warm non-alcoholic ones by those driving. The food seemed to be going down well, as full trays were coming out of the Kitchen and empty ones were going back in. There were also trays of clean plates and napkins coming out, and the dirty ones were being collected up and taken back to the Kitchen. The waitresses were certainly very efficient at their job, and there would not be a lot of clearing up for me to do at the end of the afternoon. However, I was kept busy stoking fires, refilling log

197

baskets, directing people to the facilities and helping out where needed.

It was after 4 p.m. before the first people began to leave, some of them still giggling, either from the effects of drink or remembering the lost wheel episode. As they said their goodbyes to Lord and Lady Linton I sorted through the piles of coats, making sure people were able to find the coat, hat, scarf or gloves they came in wearing. People continued to leave in dribs and drabs over the next couple of hours and by 6 p.m. the last ones had staggered out of Threldale, still giggling about the wheel episode, to make their way home.

The caterers and I were able to start clearing up, not that there was a lot to clear up. Despite the best efforts of the waitresses, though, to collect soiled glasses and plates, some were left in various quite unexpected places. It amazes me where people will put empty glasses or dirty plates if there isn't someone on hand to take it from them immediately. The two waitresses and I checked all the reception rooms for rubbish, plates and glasses. There were even some abandoned in the bathrooms.

With hardly any help from me it wasn't long before the waitresses had all the items brought by the caterers accounted for, boxed up and put in the van. The caterers, including the waitresses, left about 7 p.m., leaving Threldale empty of all signs of the funeral and subsequent refreshments.

Once they had gone I began knocking the drawing room, Dining Room, billiard room and Entrance Hall back into shape. This meant getting rid of the missed bits of rubbish still lying about (there wasn't much), removing the extra seating (there was lots), putting the furniture back in its normal positions (most had been moved), plumping cushions (they were flat), wiping down surfaces where glasses or plates had left dirty marks and giving the floors and carpets a quick sweep.

By 8 p.m. I was ready to put a light supper in the Dining Room. I had this all prepared and sitting in the pantry ready to bring up. All I had to do was set up the table in the Dining Room. By 8 30 p.m. I was done, which wasn't bad for such a big day in the life of Threldale. I had expected to finish a good deal later.

Lord and Lady Linton had disappeared as soon as the last mourner had left and retired upstairs to change and have a nap before reappearing for supper later in the evening. I hadn't seen Master Ted at all during the day but apparently he arrived on time at 11 a.m., attended the funeral with his parents, walked back with the mourners, mingled with them back at Threldale and then left at about 5 p.m. to drive back to Oxford.

All in all I think if the late Dowager Lady Linton had been looking down on the day's events she would agree that it had been a good send-off, just as she had planned. I think she would have laughed at the sight of the wheel rolling down the road too.

Trouble with Desserts

'Not tarte Tatin again!' Lady Linton lamented.

It was Sunday evening. Lord and Lady Linton had finished a roast beef dinner with roasted vegetables and Yorkshire puddings fifteen minutes earlier, and were ready for the dessert course. I had brought in the tarte Tatin with a small jug of cream and put them on the table for Lady Linton to cut up and serve. There was just the two of them home at Threldale. Master Ted was back at university in Oxford and there had been no guests for a few weeks. I had sort of slipped into a rut of housekeeping and cooking by sticking to what I knew they both liked and not trying out any new dishes. I was just pottering along enjoying the quiet mealtimes, so Lady Linton's comment jolted me out of my comfort zone.

'You really do seem to have very small repertoire of desserts, Rosie. You must expand your horizons and produce something other than the same old choices week in and week out. I am so bored with the same desserts over and over again.'

'Sorry, Lady Linton.' I thought I did provide a wide choice: apple crumble, tarte Tatin, lemon mousse, Eton mess, fruit salad, rhubarb tart, syrup sponge, custard tart … and I am sure there were others that I couldn't just bring to mind. The boredom complaint left me feeling a bit unappreciated.

'Next time we have dessert I want to see something we have not had before. Do something to excite our taste buds.'

'Yes, Lady Linton.' I had better stop being so set in my ways. She was probably right. I hadn't experimented with any new dishes for months.

I would have to get the recipe books out and look for inspiration. I am not an artistic cook, nor an imaginative one. Most of my cooking is traditional and, I would like to think, wholesome. I have to admit that while my food might taste good it would not win any prizes for presentation, but then it didn't have to. I was never going to win *MasterChef*. I didn't usually have time to take my cooking skills to that level. I cooked what I was confident with cooking and that needed to change. I had to branch out a bit.

I cleaned the Dining Room once they had finished and I noticed there was not a lot of the tarte Tatin left for a dessert they were bored with. After that I set up the room ready for breakfast the next morning, all the while thinking over what Lady Linton had said. I did a quick mental check of the various desserts I had made over the last few years and was surprised to find there were only about eight different ones that I tended to make. I really couldn't think of more than that. Maybe I was either getting stale or, more likely, just playing safe.

I got all my recipe books out on to the Kitchen table, made myself a cup of tea and spent the rest of Sunday evening reading through them looking for inspiration. By the time I closed up the hall at 10 p.m. and retired I had a list of new desserts to try over the coming weeks, and I would start with supper on the following Sunday evening.

I decided to make a sherry trifle, and I would make every layer in it from scratch. No corners would be cut. I would make my own jelly with fresh raspberry juice and gelatine and my own proper custard with eggs and cream. I would bake my own Madeira cake and soak it in a good sherry. There would be lots of fresh raspberries in the jelly, and on the top, and as a final touch, I would decorate it with a bit of spun sugar. It would be a thing of beauty.

I made the Madeira cake on the Saturday afternoon and left it cooling in the pantry overnight. On the Sunday before breakfast I cut up the cake, soaked it in sherry and put it in the bottom of crystal glass trifle bowl with some fresh raspberries. Next I made the raspberry jelly, poured it over the sponge and put the bowl in the pantry, giving it time to set. Later that morning I made the custard and poured that over the jelly. An hour later I topped it off with whipped cream, fresh raspberries and spun sugar. It was indeed, as predicted by me, a thing of beauty.

That evening after the main course of a roast chicken dinner with all the trimmings I removed the dirty dishes and brought in clean bowls and a serving spoon. I went back to the Kitchen and returned with my beautiful raspberry trifle, hoping to receive lots of praise considering the amount of work I had put into it.

'So what have you come up with, Rosie?' Lady Linton asked, expectantly.

'A raspberry trifle, Lady Linton,' I proudly replied, pointing at my creation on the sideboard.

'A trifle. Not exactly difficult to make, and hardly a dessert that requires any imagination.' This was not the response I was expecting, and I felt quite deflated.

'No, Lady Linton, but it is something I haven't made before.'

'That's true. Well, let's see if it lives up to expectations.'

'Yes, Lady Linton.' I left her to serve up the trifle to Lord Linton and herself and returned to the Kitchen not nearly as buoyant as I had been when I took the trifle into the Dining Room. I didn't have a good feeling any more about this dessert.

I sat at the Kitchen table, waited for twenty minutes and then went back up to the Dining Room to receive the verdict.

'It was a nice enough trifle but not one I think we can add to the list of future dessert options, Rosie. It isn't as if there is any skill in making one. I would expect it to be served to a child in a nursery rather than as an option on a supper party menu. You need not repeat it.'

To say I was disappointed would be an under-statement. I thought everyone loved a trifle but I had to go with Lady Linton's judgement and cross trifle off the list of possible additional dessert options. I also had a sherry trifle with two scoops out of it and I was not going to get away with serving it up after lunch the next day. I wasn't going to waste it. I would offer it to Sam and Don as a special tea break treat and I would take some of it myself to have after my own evening meal.

Over the next few weeks I tried a variety of different desserts with varying degrees of success. The sequence of events was the same for each new dessert I presented. On Sunday, after the main course, I would bring in the new dish from the Kitchen and place it on the sideboard, telling Lady Linton what it was. I would leave the Dining Room for twenty minutes to allow her to inspect my efforts, serve up two portions on to dessert plates, consume my offering and reach a verdict. After that time I would return to find out what Lady Linton thought of the dessert and whether it was to be approved or dismissed.

The crème brûlée with shortbread biscuits was a great success, which surprised me, as I thought that might be considered too simple a dish because it is only a creamy custard with a brittle caramel seal. Not so. Lady Linton liked it being served in individual dishes and loved breaking the brittle caramel on top. Shortbread already had her approval as a dessert accompaniment. I was surprised but pleased at the verdict. Approved.

The profiteroles with a hot chocolate sauce did not

meet with approval. Lady Linton thought, as a dessert, it lacked the finesse she was looking for when having guests to supper and that hot chocolate sauce might be a bit too messy, should it drip on to the clothes of dining guests. I was a bit surprised, as I really thought this one would be a winner. I thought it impossible to produce a chocolate dessert that wouldn't be liked. Dismissed.

The cherry *clafoutis* with vanilla ice cream was another failure. Lady Linton declared it far too heavy a dessert to have after a large meal, and that it lacked a certain presence at the dining table. She found the sponge heavy, the cherries too tart, and feared cherry juice stains on cherished garments. Dismissed.

The lemon tart with raspberry coulis went down a storm. Lady Linton liked any dessert with lemons in it so I knew this one would be a success. The raspberry coulis was a gamble, considering the previous comments regarding accidental spills. Another gamble was not serving cream with it. However, this one was Lady Linton's favourite of all the new desserts I offered for her delectation. Approved.

The chocolate fondants with Chantilly cream received a big tick, partly because the liquid centre made it look like a clever pudding. Until I made this dessert for the first time I had only ever served plain old fresh cream with dessert. The Chantilly cream was something new. As for the fondants, I just hoped I would get the timing right every time I made it. There is nothing worse than a fondant with a set centre. Approved.

The sticky toffee pudding with toffee sauce met with the approval of them both. Lord Linton declared this to be his new favourite dessert and stated that it must be added to the list of new desserts. Luckily Lady Linton loved the dessert too. I served this as a single large pudding but was able to inform Lady Linton that it could easily be made as individual puddings, which pleased her even more. Approved.

The tiramisu was an absolute disaster. As far as Lady Linton was concerned this was just a coffee trifle in disguise, and the fact that it was an Italian classic mattered not a jot. She was convinced I had just produced another trifle with different flavours and given it a foreign name. Dismissed.

The treacle tart with vanilla ice cream was loved by both Lord and Lady Linton and duly added to the growing list of new desserts. When making this one I had some serious doubts about it as it seemed too simple and old-fashioned a dessert but I was pleasantly surprised by their positive reaction. Approved.

The queen of puddings served with fresh cream was approved as a pudding that should be on every list of desserts. Lady Linton couldn't understand why I had never made such a classic before. This was her verdict as soon as I brought it in and told her what it was before she had even tried it. Her opinion didn't change after after having eaten it. Approved.

The chocolate chip bread and butter pudding received praise as being a clever and quite grown-up variation of an old nursery pudding. I nearly didn't do this one as it reminded me too much of school dinners, and I was worried that Lady Linton would regard it as too childish. How wrong was I? Approved.

I now had an additional seven new desserts to add to my existing repertoire of eight desserts. I had quite enjoyed myself experimenting over the previous weeks and promised to myself to continue looking for fresh ideas. In fact I thought I might start looking through my recipe books at new possibilities for first courses and even main courses. Lady Linton had woken me out of my cooking doldrums. Maybe it was time to shake things up a bit and experiment, when meals were just for Lord and Lady Linton. I certainly couldn't experiment when they had a supper party.

Lady Linton was keen to show off the new dessert choices, and to this end she told me she had guests coming for supper in a couple of days' time and wanted me to make the lemon tart with a raspberry coulis for the dessert course. This was one of the new options that I had lots of confidence about making, despite only having made it once. The starter, which was smoked salmon and prawn pâté with Melba toast, and the main course, which was rack of lamb with Pommes Anna and vegetables, were tried and tested dishes, so I didn't feel under any particular pressure in preparing those.

The night of the supper party arrived, as did the guests for supper. After drinks and chatting, everyone moved from the drawing room through to the Dining Room and settled down to enjoy an evening of good food in amiable company. The starter was served, eaten and removed, as was the main course. A wine compatible with the each of the dishes was selected and poured by Lord Linton. Everyone was relaxed and enjoying themselves. So now it was time for the new dessert of lemon tart with raspberry coulis.

I carefully lifted the tart out of the fridge, eased it out of the baking tin on to a serving plate and sifted a layer of icing sugar over the top. I transferred the coulis from the pan on the Kitchen table, where it had been cooling, into a rather pretty glass jug. Before taking the tart through to the Dining Room I took in the dessert plates and the raspberry coulis and put them on the sideboard ready for serving. I then returned to the Kitchen to get the lemon tart.

Back in the Kitchen, I looked at the beautiful creation that was the lemon tart before picking the serving plate up off the table and going out into the passage and along to the Entrance Hall. With great pride I entered the Dining Room and – disaster – I missed my footing on the edge of the carpet. In trying not to fall I tilted the serving plate with the tart on it. It all seemed to happen in slow motion. As I fell forward, trying to regain my balance with the serving plate tilting at an alarming angle, the tart slid off, turned over in mid-air and hit the Dining Room carpet upside down with a splat.

I managed to regain my balance and stand up straight. It was then I looked at the tart spread across the carpet in many pieces and then looked at Lady Linton's horrified expression … and looked back at the mess that had been the tart. As I stood there dumfounded I knew this was not going to end well. I could feel the colour rise in my face and I actually felt like crying at the destruction of my creation. In all my ten years at Threldale I had never dropped anything in front of guests, much less something I was so proud of.

Lady Linton quickly regained her composure and fixed me with a stare that was so icy I could feel my blood running cold.

'Rosie, I think you need to clear away that mess. We will retire to the drawing room while you do so.' Had there not been guests present I think she would have said more. She stood up and ushered her guests away from the dining table, around the disaster on the carpet and out of the door. I hovered to one side with my head down to let everyone pass, aware of the eyes of Lady Linton boring into me and my face burning with acute embarrassment.

I knelt down, picked up the bigger pieces and put them back on the serving plate. I then used the cake slice to scoop up the rest of the tart, trying not to squish it into the carpet any more than it already had been. I took the whole sorry pile back to the Kitchen, threw it in the bin and put the plate into the sink. There was no way any of it could be salvaged. It was not only squashed and broken, it was now full of carpet fibres too. Next, I took a bowl of soapy water and a clean cloth into the Dining Room and set to, cleaning the remaining mess out of the carpet. If crying would have fixed the problem then I would have cried. However, that is not me. I cleaned up the mess, picked myself up in the process, put my shoulders back and moved on.

At some point I was going to have to face Lady Linton, but hopefully not until the guests had gone.

As it was I didn't see or hear from her for the rest of the evening, so once I was sure the guests had left I locked up and retired to my little flat with some trepidation about what the following day would bring. At least Lady Linton would have had time to cool down.

The next day I finished cleaning up the last of the crockery, the cutlery and the pots from the supper party of the night before and set up breakfast in the Dining Room. The carpet was now dry, and clean of all signs of the mess from the night before. Once all that was done I waited in the Kitchen for the inevitable summons from Lady Linton. It came at ten thirty as she came down to breakfast.

'Rosie, come through to the Dining Room, now.' No please or thank you. I was in big trouble. I followed her into the room.

'Yesterday a lovely evening was completely ruined by carelessness on your part. Do you have an explanation for what happened?' She was looking at me with steel in her eyes.

'No, Lady Linton, I don't. I lost my footing on the carpet in the doorway but I have no idea how or why.'

'Is there a problem with the carpet there?'

'No, Lady Linton.'

'Was it dark by the doorway?'

'No, Lady Linton.'

'In that case I can see no reason why you should have tripped unless you just weren't paying attention. I am very disappointed in you, Rosie.'

'Yes, Lady Linton.'

'Did you manage to save any of the tart?'

'No, Lady Linton.'

'We can ill afford such wastage.'

'No, Lady Linton.'

'It was my particular favourite of the new desserts. I expect you to take a great deal more care in future. For now the incident is closed but do not think it is forgotten. You may go back to your duties.'

'Yes, Lady Linton.' I was glad that was over. It could have been a lot worse.

Thinking on the whole debacle a few days later when emotions had calmed down, I think Lady Linton was more embarrassed by my accident with the tart than by the loss of the tart itself. It made me feel better to think of the incident in those terms anyway.

I have made the lemon tart with raspberry coulis many times since then but I have not dropped it again. I am even able to laugh at the mental picture I have of the lemon tart sliding majestically off the plate and on to the floor. Even the splat sound makes me laugh.

It Was the Fairies

(O)ne of the more taxing issues of working at Threld-ale was the absent-mindedness of both Lord and Lady Linton. Things were put down and forgotten then thought to be lost or moved by some unknown person. This happened so many times over the years that I had to develop a routine for finding the missing item before tempers got frayed or minds drifted off on to other things, depending on who had lost the offending item.

If it was Lady Linton who had lost, misplaced or just plain moved something, then this involved first of all allowing her to have her say for as long as it took her to run out of steam. I learnt over the years not to interrupt, as this just prolonged the tirade. It was better to wait in silence. She would blame Lord Linton, Sam or Don, me or, as the final culprit, the fairies. She rarely admitted to having lost anything, and was adamant that somebody else must have lost it, moved it or taken it. She would insist it was left in a particular place and it wasn't there now. If no one owned up to moving whatever it was then that is when she would be heard to to declare,

'Well, the fairies must have moved it!'

So, when Lady Linton had her say, I would then systematically check around those rooms most used by her, looking for the said missing item. While I was doing this Lady Linton would be unsystematically and randomly throwing things off chairs and tables in one room before repeating the process in another room in her own search for the offending item, and would often revisit rooms and throw things back on to chairs and tables. She would also tell me I was wasting my time looking in a particular place as she had already looked there, though quite often that was exactly where the missing item was.

Patience, persistence and a system on my part usually turned up whatever it was. I would return the item to Lady Linton, who usually insisted she had not put it wherever it was found by declaring,

'It must be the fairies!'

I would then just carry on with my duties. I had had this happen so many times with bags, correspondence, books, ornaments, items of clothing, and pretty much anything small enough to be handled and therefore easily lost or misplaced.

A good example of this would be Lady Linton's secateurs. They were very old and very rusty but she swore that nothing was sharper than they were and that modern ones were not made anything like as well as her trusty old pair. The gardeners had several pairs of newer, shinier, sharper secateurs, but as far as Lady Linton was concerned they were useless.

The rule with her secateurs was that no one – but no

213

one – was allowed to use them, move them or touch them in case they should go missing. They sat in a basket on the table in the Entrance Hall so everyone knew where they were and nobody touched them – not Lord Linton, not Sam or Don – and certainly not me. We all valued a life of peace and quiet, and where possible did nothing to upset Lady Linton.

One warm and bright summer's day, after having had her lunch, Lady Linton decided the time had come to do some pruning in the garden. Whether Sam and Don would appreciate her helping in a task they normally carried out or not is another matter. She tended to use the scattergun approach to anything she tackled in the garden, and no task was ever left in a finished state. Sam and Don were used to having to complete whatever it was she had started.

So she donned her gardening clothes, which consisted of an old tweed skirt, a faded blouse, a slightly threadbare cardigan, a grubby-looking coat, a sun hat and a pair of gardening gloves. She considered gardening to be a job that required the correct old attire to do it in.

She took the keys from the key cupboard in the Entrance Hall and put them in the pocket of her coat. These keys were for the battered old golf buggy that was used for getting around the estate grounds. Finally she picked up the basket from the hall table and checked it contained her gardening equipment, including her precious secateurs. That was when the disappearance was discovered.

'Rosie! Rosie! Have you moved my secateurs?' she

called to me through the door to the passage to the Kitchen.

'Coming, Lady Linton.' I pushed through the door, wiping flour from my hands. I was in the middle of kneading a pile of bread dough prior to making a number of loaves of bread for the freezer and had hoped to be left in peace to complete the task.

'Well, have you?'

'Sorry, Lady Linton, I didn't hear what you said.' My hearing is pretty good, but while I had heard her voice when I was in the Kitchen I hadn't been able to discern what she had actually said.

'My secateurs are missing out of the basket. Have you moved them?' She looked at me accusingly.

'No, Lady Linton.'

'Well, someone has and if it wasn't you then I suppose it must have been the fairies.' This was the standard response for when things went missing. It was always the fairies if no other explanation was available. It was never goblins or pixies or unicorns. No, it was always the fairies.

'I will have a look around and see if I can find them,' I replied. My bread making was going to have to wait until the secateurs were found. Lady Linton would not rest until they were back in her basket, and if she did not rest then neither did I.

'It is completely pointless you looking for them as I have already done that,' she insisted. However, I was fairly certain that wasn't true but said nothing.

'A second pair of eyes sometimes helps, Lady Linton,' I replied diplomatically.

'Well, if you want to waste your time go ahead, but I have already searched everywhere in the house and they are not here. Someone has taken them despite my express wish that no one should touch them. They are the only decent secateurs we have.'

I headed for the drawing room to begin my search. I could hear Lady Linton mumbling to herself as she emptied the basket to check the secateurs definitely weren't there. I then heard her footsteps heading towards the Library. She was obviously going to enquire whether Lord Linton had taken them. I had never known him do any gardening of any description, so it was highly unlikely that he was the culprit.

I carried on looking in the drawing room, checking all the places Lady Linton was likely to have been in the last few hours. I worked my way around the room slowly and methodically, but to no avail. At least I was sure the secateurs were not in the drawing room. I moved on to the Entrance Hall and carried out the same exercise and again drew a blank. This was proving to be a bit of a puzzle.

I saw Lady Linton come out of the Library not looking any happier, and head towards the front door. I think she was about to go out to quiz the gardeners, though why she should think they would take them is beyond me when they had several pairs of their own. It was at this point that I noticed something odd about the gardening coat that she was wearing. I was almost certain I could see one of the pockets bulging ominously. Something told me that this bulge was the missing secateurs. She must have put them in her pocket instead of the basket the last time she used them. Now that I thought I knew where they were how was I going get Lady Linton to check her pockets?

'Lady Linton,' I said as I endeavoured to get her attention.

'What now? Can't you see I'm busy? I need to go and speak to Sam or Don. Have you found my secateurs?'

'No, Lady Linton.'

'Well, in that case, don't interrupt me while I, at least, try to find out who that has taken them.'

'But, Lady Linton, I think I may know where they are.'

'What! How can you know unless you put them there? Tell me, then! Don't just stand there.'

'I think they may be in the pocket of your gardening coat.'

'Don't be ridiculous! Don't you think I would have checked there in the first place?'

'Please, Lady Linton, will you have another look?' She looked at me, sighed with exasperation and put her hand in her coat pocket, more to satisfy me than because she thought they might actually be there.

'What? Oh! How did they get there? They certainly weren't there ten minutes ago. Did you put them there when I wasn't looking?'

'No, Lady Linton.' I looked at her incredulously.

'Well, if it wasn't you, it must have been the fairies who put them in my pocket because I definitely did not.'

She removed them from her pocket, put them back

217

in her basket and left by the front door. I watched her climb on to the buggy and head off across the front lawns, perched majestically on the driving seat. She would probably vent her frustration on a shrub somewhere, snipping it to within an inch of its life. I hoped Sam and Don would give her a wide berth until she had finished venting her frustration on the plant life in the grounds. If there are any fairies in the bottom of the garden at Threldale they must spend most of their time hiding from Lady Linton.

Now, if it was Lord Linton who had lost something, he was inclined to be less prickly about it and tended not to blame the fairies, or anyone else for that matter, for either losing the item or finding it. With Lord Linton the problem was finding whatever it was before he forgot he was looking for it and had moved on to something else. More than once I found an item that he had misplaced, only to be told by him that he didn't know it was lost. This could be very frustrating for my part, especially if I had spent a lot of time looking for it.

An example of this was his favourite pair of gold cufflinks, which had a blue and white enamelled inset in a chessboard design. They had been a gift from Lady Linton on their wedding day many years ago and were of great sentimental value to him. He had at least half a dozen other pairs of cufflinks, but the gold pair were the ones he wore the most.

One morning he arrived down to breakfast with the cuffs of his shirt undone and flapping below the ends of the sleeves of his jacket, which made him look rather untidy as a result. He usually arrived in the Dining Room immaculately turned out first thing each day, and was very particular about his appearance.

'I say, Rosie, I seem to have misplaced my favourite enamelled cufflinks. I want to wear them today when I go into York to meet with the accountants this morning. Any chance you can work one of your miracles and find them for me?'

'Yes, Lord Linton.' No accusations, just a polite request.

'I remember wearing them yesterday but I can't seem to find them this morning,' he said, sitting down at his place and pouring himself a coffee and picking up his morning newspaper.

'I'll take a look while you are having your breakfast, Lord Linton.'

'Good. Much appreciated,' he said, as he began helping himself to toast and marmalade.

I excused myself and headed straight upstairs to his dressing room. This small room was part of his bedroom suite, which consisted of his bedroom, a bathroom, a walk-in wardrobe, a dressing room and a connecting corridor. All his pairs of cufflinks were kept in a wooden box made for that purpose. Inside there was a red velvet-lined compartment for each pair, and this box lived on the top of a large chest of drawers in his dressing room. Every night, when undressing for bed, Lord Linton would take off his cufflinks and put them in the appropriate compartment of the box for that pair. He was a creature of habit, so it was unusual for him to have misplaced his favourite pair.

I checked the obvious place first, the wooden box, and the cufflinks he wanted weren't there. The compartment that normally held them was empty. All the others were in their individual compartments. So when he took them off last night he must have put them down somewhere in one of the rooms that made up his bedroom suite. Time to go around each of the rooms in turn. I knew he had worn them the day before as I had seen them myself on his shirt. Surely they couldn't be too difficult to find.

It took me a good half hour to go around all the rooms in turn, starting in the dressing room. There was no sign of the offending cufflinks. At this rate Lord Linton would have finished his breakfast and would then want to leave for York.

As a final check I got on my hands and knees to peer under the various pieces of furniture, again going around each of the rooms in turn. Bingo! There they were under the bed in his bedroom.

He must have put them on his bedside table and then knocked them off it when removing his shirt. I fished them out from their dusty hiding place and, rather than take them downstairs to him, I went through to his dressing room to put them back in the wooden box in the correct compartment. Feeling rather pleased with myself, I went downstairs to inform Lord Linton of my success. Hoping he was still breakfasting, I went into the Dining Room. But, unsurprisingly, he was no longer in there. I could see from the used dishes at his place that he had eaten breakfast and, from the way it was spread about, that he had read the morning paper. I left the Dining Room and went across to the Library, knocked on the door and popped my head in. He wasn't in there either. Next I tried the drawing room and drew another blank. Only Lady Linton was in there, reading her morning paper and drinking her coffee. When she looked up I apologised for disturbing her and left, closing the door behind me. This was getting silly. Where on earth had he got to?

As I came out of the drawing room I saw his back disappearing upstairs. I was not about to follow him upstairs. We all need some privacy. I would have to wait until he came downstairs again before I could tell him of my success in finding his cufflinks.

While I was waiting I made a start on clearing away the used breakfast things in the Dining Room. It was less than ten minutes later that I heard Lord Linton coming down the stairs. I stopped what I was doing and headed out into the Entrance Hall to try and catch him before he left. He was standing in the hall, his briefcase in one hand and his coat over his other arm, looking thoughtful. I wondered if he was thinking about his lost cufflinks.

'Lord Linton, about your lost cufflinks,' I called to attract his attention.

'What cufflinks? I haven't lost any cufflinks.' He came out of his reverie and looked at me quite puzzled.

'The blue and while enamelled ones,' I reminded him.

'No, I haven't lost them. I have just got them out of the box and put them on.' He really had no idea that he had lost them or that he had asked me to look for them.

'Yes, Lord Linton. I found them under your bed and put them back in the box.'

'When did you do that? I thought I put them back in the box last night.'

'Don't worry about it, Lord Linton. As long as they are on your shirt that is all that matters. Have a nice day in York.'

'Thank you, Rosie, I will.'

Typical. He had totally forgotten that he had lost them or that he had sent me in search of them. At least he was leaving for York a happy man, with his favourite cufflinks on his shirt. The added bonus for me was that I didn't get the blame and neither did the fairies.

The Dressing Room

$\mathcal{L}$ord and Lady Linton had separate sleeping arrangements, and had had for years. Their suites were opposite each other on the first floor of Threldale Hall and were mirrors of each other, both with views restricted to the rear courtyard and the old stables.

Lord Linton's suite reflected his personality and had a very masculine air about it. He had a place for everything and liked it kept tidy. Being a bit absent-minded it made it easier for him to keep track of things, so long as he put things back where they belonged, of course.

Now I was always able to get into his suite and and give it a good tidy-up, clean the bathroom, change the bedding, hang up his discarded clothing, collect his dirty laundry and return various items such as shoes, belts and cufflinks to their rightful places. It was kept well dusted, polished and vacuumed. No, Lord Linton's private suite was never a problem.

Lady Linton's private suite was altogether another matter. She was untidy but still knew where every single item was. She never threw anything out so there was not an inch of space to spare, especially in her dressing room. She could be very prickly about anything she considered to be an invasion of her privacy. These rooms were her domain where she could totally relax and keep all her private treasures, whatever they happened to be. She did not like me going in there, which made my job rather difficult.

This desire for privacy dated back to a housekeeper who had worked for the family a long way before my time. Rumour had it that this predecessor of mine was apt to pry where she shouldn't and then gossip to anyone who would listen about what she found. Lady Linton had discovered this and felt betrayed, and as a result she struggled to fully trust her housekeeper. And unfortunately that was now me.

I sympathised with her feelings. There weren't many places in Threldale that she could truly call private. It had taken me many years to work out what my boundaries were when cleaning her suite. Basically ... stay out. There were still times when I had to go in, to change the bed linen or towels, for example, and she always knew when I had been in no matter how hard I tried to leave the rooms exactly as I had found them – minus the dirty laundry, of course. As part of my routine I tried desperately not to touch or move anything I thought to be of a personal nature, but inevitably she still thought I had. So I always entered her suite with care and caution uppermost in my mind.

Such was the case when I decided that Lady Linton's rooms smelt a bit musty and stale, and I really needed to give them a good spring clean. It had been well over a year since I had last been able to clean them, and that had been quite cursory. My normal daily routine in these rooms was restricted to steering a central path that enabled me to empty bins, scoop up dirty laundry, remove dirty dishes and change the bedding.

Dusting was a near impossible task, and it annoyed my inner housekeeper that dust lay thick on every surface of every piece of furniture in every room. There was also the issue of ring marks, lots of them, where she kept her perfumes, creams, bath oils and cosmetics. Some of them were quite thick and sticky. What lay behind and under all the clutter I dreaded to think. There could be all sorts of bugs living and breeding in the darkest corners.

I really needed to deep clean the rooms and get them smelling sweeter. I hatched a plan of action. And to head off any adverse comments I would take it a room at a time, starting with the one least likely to upset her – the bathroom. Once a room was complete I would tell Lady Linton what I had done and then gently soothe her before tackling the next one after a week or two had passed and she had calmed down.

So, on a quiet day, I took my cleaning box and cloths upstairs to her suite while she was out visiting friends. I set to in the bathroom and started scrubbing the bath, the shower, the basin and the tiling and removed months of black mould, scum and hair, and the dried-up remnants of shampoo, soap and bubble bath. This was followed by the chrome fittings, which were difficult to see under all the limescale. By the time I had finished everything positively gleamed.

Next on the agenda was the frosted bathroom window. The glass and frame were thick with cobwebs, black mould and green slime, I couldn't remember when I had last been able to get into the bathroom to clean it this deep. Luckily there were no curtains or blinds to worry about. By the time I had finished the windows my cleaning cloths were only fit for the bin. I would need to use clean ones for the next job.

I had been putting off cleaning the shelving that held Lady Linton's perfumes, lotions, potions, cosmetics and medication. There were also cotton wool balls, make-up removal pads, cotton buds, brushes, combs, hair clips and other paraphernalia. There were two stands against the wall, each with six shelves. Every shelf was filled to capacity, and I don't know how she could find anything. This was going to be tricky … taking the items off and wiping them, cleaning each shelf and putting them back exactly where they came from.

I took a deep breath and began with the top shelf on the first stand. I studied where every item was before removing it and placing it on the floor on a mock-up shelf in a replicated position. Some of the items took a bit of removing as they were stuck fast to the glass shelf, but perseverance got every item loose. Once it was empty the shelf was removed, washed in soapy water, dried, put back in place, and the items were then replaced on the shelf as I had found them. I repeated the exercise for the remaining five shelves and then moved on to the second stand. It took me a couple of hours just to do this one job but to my eye the shelves on both stands looked the same as before I started, just cleaner.

That just left the floor, the walls and the skirtings, which took me a lot less time to clean than the shelving had done. I surveyed my handiwork and was pleased at how clean the bathroom looked and smelt. Now I had to hope that Lady Linton would be equally pleased once I gently broke the news to her that I had deep cleaned her bathroom.

When she returned, just fifteen minutes after I had finished, she headed straight up to her private suite to change. I was unable to intercept her so I hadn't been able to tell her what I had done, all I could do was hold my breath and wait.

'Rosie, come up here a minute.' Lady Linton summoned me upstairs. I think she had worked it out for herself.

'Yes, Lady Linton.' I couldn't tell whether she was happy with what I had done or not.

'Rosie, have you been moving things in my bathroom?'

'Yes, Lady Linton. I've deep cleaned it.'

'I thought so. Nothing is in the place where I left it. I had better be able to still find everything. I hope you haven't thrown anything out. You know how I hate my things being touched.'

'Yes, Lady Linton.'

'Everything certainly looks cleaner now, but I must insist that you ask me before coming into my rooms to clean.'

'Yes, Lady Linton.' It was going to be tricky cleaning the other rooms, but now I'd started I was determined to finish.

So, despite me thinking I had put everything back exactly where I had found it, she still knew I had been in there. At least she hadn't lost her temper or completely barred me from going into her rooms. I decided that, all in all, it had been a positive outcome.

Over the next couple of weeks I worked on the connecting passage and the bedroom. I cleaned the skirtings, wiped the walls, vacuumed and cleaned the carpets, pulled out the furniture so I could clean behind it and washed and polished the windows and window frames. I managed to do it all without incurring the wrath of Lady Linton, though she did get a little grumpy. She still passed comment about me not having asked permission to enter her rooms and having moved things, and insisted on checking I hadn't lost or thrown out anything precious. Each time she also begrudgingly admitted the rooms that had been cleaned looked better for my efforts.

That just left the dressing room and the walk-in wardrobe. I couldn't even think about starting these rooms if there was the slightest chance of her interrupting me. Lady Linton considered these rooms to be her most private. Knowing her as I did, and knowing her reservations about housekeepers and snooping, I would have to be very careful when cleaning. I know that if she did catch me she would stop me in my tracks, convinced that I would misplace or lose something valuable. I hoped she knew me well enough to know that I would not abuse the trust she placed in me by snooping, as my predecessor had done many years ago.

As it turned out Lady Linton received an invitation from an old friend to attend a concert in London and to stay the night after the performance. She planned to leave straight after breakfast and catch the morning train from York down to London. It would be late afternoon the following day before she returned to Threldale.

This was my chance to finish cleaning her suite.

On the day Lady Linton left to get her train I waited until I was sure there was no chance of her returning because she had forgotten something vital for her trip. I had the rest of the day and the next morning to completely finish the job before she returned the following afternoon.

I gathered up all my cleaning equipment, cloths, cleaning fluids, brushes and vacuum, and headed upstairs to start. I decided the dressing room would be slightly easier than the walk-in wardrobe. This room was big enough to be a double bedroom in anyone else's home, though the amount of furniture and personal possessions in it made it look a lot smaller.

Opposite the door was a huge floor-to-ceiling window letting in swathes of sunshine. To the right of the window was a dressing table strewn with brushes, combs, jewellery, make-up and skin creams with a chair facing the mirror and a metal bin under the table. To the left was a writing desk stacked high with open correspondence, pens, writing paper, cards and envelopes, all awaiting Lady Linton's attention. It also had a chair in front of it and a wastepaper basket. Behind the door on the right was an antique and rather battered daybed. This had disappeared under a huge pile of clothes, which spilt on to the floor. On the left of the room was an armchair and an occasional table in front of a fireplace. Finally there was a large log basket to one side of the fire and a set of fire irons on a stand to the other.

I would take this room a section at a time, making a careful note of where everything was before moving a single item, and starting out from the left of the door and moving clockwise around the room. Before I could even do that I needed to remove the tray of dirty dishes from the table in front of the fire and take them down to the Kitchen. I also needed to empty the bins. There were four of them altogether: one by the dressing table, one by the writing desk, one by the armchair and one by the daybed. All four of them were full to overflowing with discarded correspondence, old newspapers, empty cosmetic pots and other unidentifiable rubbish.

Now I was ready to begin. I studied the first section to the left of the door and round to the fireplace, mentally noting where to put things back when I had finished. I removed the clutter from the table, the armchair and the mantel over the fireplace and put it down in order on the floor of the corridor outside the room. Next I also moved all the smaller items of furniture and fittings out into the corridor until I had a clear floor space.

The fluff and dust revealed had to be seen to be believed. I wiped down all the washable surfaces, polished the furniture, then vacuumed and cleaned that section of the carpet. Taking my time, I carefully put everything back in place, giving it all a good wipe with a damp cloth first. It looked so much better. It showed just how dusty and grimy the rest of the room was. I couldn't stop now I had started.

I repeated this exercise three more times. Each time seemed to take longer than the previous time as each successive quarter was more cluttered than the previous one. I have to admit to not touching Lady Linton's writing desk. There was just too much personal correspondence on there, and I was keen to prove to her that I didn't snoop.

By the time I had been right round the room and reached the door again I was tired and dirty, but hugely satisfied at finally having being able clean the room. As far as I could see the only difference between how the suite looked before and after was the absence of dirt. Whether Lady Linton would agree with me would be something I would find out on her return. This had taken me all morning and some of the afternoon. It was now 3 p.m.

Before starting on the walk-in wardrobe I stopped to clean myself up and make myself a late lunch. I was ravenous after my morning's exertions. I was lucky that Lord Linton was out as well, so I didn't have any lunches to prepare other than my own. He would be back for supper later, so I would have to bear that in mind and keep an eye on the time. An hour later I was ready for round two and headed back upstairs to tackle the biggest job of all, Lady Linton's walk-in wardrobe.

This was quite a small room, long and narrow with hanging rails on either side, shoe racks underneath, and floor-to-ceiling drawers on the facing wall at the end. Nothing seemed to be in its right place. Clothes were hung up askew, barely even on the hangers. Shoes weren't paired in the shoe rack or lined up straight, and clothes spilt out of the drawers. The piles of clothes on the floor seemed to be inside out or scrunched up, and I wasn't even sure if they were all clean. This was going to be a huge task. How on earth was I going to get this room clean and leave it looking like I had never even touched anything?

Due to the shape of the walk-in wardrobe I couldn't clean this one section at a time. I would have to start at the front, after moving stuff into the corridor. Then I would have to set it out in order on the floor and work my way to the back. I should finish up with everything in order on the floor out in the corridor, which would make it easier for me to put everything back as I found it. It was going to take me several hours to do this and I couldn't rush it.

The temptation to separate out dirty laundry, straighten up shoes, rehang garments and fold up items in the drawers was very strong, but that really would have landed me in trouble. I knelt down on the floor and began to clear the floor space one item at a time out into the corridor. It took a while, but once the floor was clear I was able to get at the bottoms of the wardrobes to clean them. I moved the shoes out of the shoe racks and into the corridor.

The bottoms of the wardrobes were now clear enough to clean. I swept out the dirt that had dropped off various shoes and boots – and the dead spiders and the flies, and other unidentifiable rubbish – to reveal a rather grubby surface, which I then wiped down with a warm soapy cloth. I could now reach the drawers at the back, and rather than disturb any of the garments hanging out higgledy-piggledy I just wiped down the front of the drawers. There was not a lot else I could do without upsetting Lady Linton.

The final job was to vacuum the floor. It all looked clean and tidy and it seemed a shame to have to put everything back. However, I did carefully put it all back as I had found it, starting at the end where the drawers were and working my way forward. Although I knew it was all clean it didn't look any better due to the amount of clutter I had to put back on the floor. It really was difficult not tidying up. It went against my housekeeping instincts.

I stood in the corridor, stretched out my back and looked around me at all the rooms I had cleaned over the last few weeks. I had done it. Lady Linton's entire suite was clean – well, as clean as I could get it with the amount of stuff I had to work around. I looked at the time. It was 7.30 p.m. It had taken me three and a half hours to clean a wardrobe! I needed to get cleaned up and think about Lord Linton's supper. It would have to be something simple, given the late hour. He was usually happy with whatever was out in front of him, and I did have a couple of options in the fridge that just needed sticking in the oven to cook.

Now I had to wait until Lady Linton returned to see whether or not she approved of my efforts. I felt like I had worked hard and that before I went to bed that night I needed a long, hot bath to soak away all the dust and to ease my aching muscles. My clothes were now more than a little grubby. I would have to put them all in the laundry and put on fresh ones tomorrow.

Lady Linton returned to Threldale the following afternoon, having thoroughly enjoyed her sojourn in London. She dropped her bags in the Entrance Hall and headed straight upstairs to her rooms to take off her coat and shoes. I braced myself for the inevitable summons, and it came less than minute after she entered her dressing room.

'Rosie! Rosie! Can you come here a moment?'

'Yes, Lady Linton.' I hurried upstairs and went into the lion's den.

'Have you been cleaning in here?'

'Yes, Lady Linton, but I made sure everything was put back exactly where you left it.'

'Have you been cleaning anywhere else?'

'Yes, your wardrobe.'

'I really must insist that you do not clean my rooms unless I specifically ask you to.'

'Yes, Lady Linton.'

'You know I have a system in place so that I know where everything is. You had better hope that I can find where things are. I will have to spend the rest of today checking nothing is missing. I was hoping to relax after my tiring train journey.'

'Sorry, Lady Linton.' I wasn't really. It needed doing, and a bit of earache was worth it.

'Next time check with me first. I'll have coffee in here while I am sorting what you have done.' I considered myself dismissed and went to fetch her a coffee tray.

Now I could lie and say I would never clean Lady Linton's rooms without her express permission, but I won't. I knew that in future I would to have use the same devious means to do my job. A housekeeper has gotta do what a housekeeper has gotta do.

Sheets and Duvets

*A*ll the beds at Threldale Hall were made up with cotton sheets, woollen blankets and feather pillows. Not only was this quite old-fashioned in the new millennium, but all the bedding had come out of the ark. The sheets were very patched and had stains of unknown origin in places, the blankets were so threadbare that daylight could be seen through them, and the feathers in the pillows had broken down such a long time ago that the contents must just be dust. I would not have liked to have spent even a single night sleeping under any of the Threldale bedding.

Every year I tried to persuade Lady Linton to buy new sheets and pillows and to change to duvets and duvet covers but every year she refused on the grounds that there was nothing wrong with sheets and blankets. She was also of the opinion that the pillows had plenty of life left in them yet, and that was what bothered me. It might be the creepy-crawly sort of life. Sheets and blankets I could wash, but it wasn't as easy to do that with pillows.

As the year progressed from the chill of winter to the early warmth of spring I removed the extra winter blankets from the beds and decided it was time to try again, but this time I was not going to do it alone. Master Ted was currently home from university for the Easter recess and I knew he used fluffy pillows and a duvet on the bed he used in the flat he occupied when studying up at Oxford. This meant he was already a fan of duvets, and so I saw him as an ally.

Master Ted had already passed a comment to me that he was thinking about bringing his own bedding from the flat when he came home for the summer to Threldale as he found the sheets and blankets on his bed uncomfortable, smelly, itchy and cold. He owed me a favour after the debacle that his shooting weekend had turned out to be the previous November, when he and his friends had made such a mess that it had taken me weeks to clean it all up.

So one morning when he came down for breakfast, long after Lord and Lady Linton had had theirs, I made my approach.

'Excuse me, Master Ted, can I have a word?'

'Of course, Rosie. What can I do for you?'

'I think the time may have come for Threldale to restock with new bed linen, but I am not sure how to approach or persuade Lady Linton. While I may be able to convince her of the need for new sheets and the like, I am not sure I can convince her of the benefits of moving from blankets to duvets. I was hoping you may drop a few hints on my behalf.'

'What a good idea. I hate the pillows and blankets we have here. They are so old, smelly and old-fashioned. Leave it with me, and I will see what I can do to get Mama thinking that it is the best thing to do.'

'Thank you, Master Ted.' I left it at that. If Master Ted couldn't move his mother's preference from sheets and blankets to duvets then all hope was lost.

It was a couple of weeks later when Master Ted approached me late one afternoon when I was working in the Dining Room. He came into the room and closed the door behind him, all very cloak-and-dagger. He was due to go back to Oxford the next day, so I wondered what it was he wanted to talk to me about.

'Rosie, I am glad I caught you. I have been discussing bed linen with Mama, telling her how much I prefer my duvet and crisp bed linen at the flat and how uncomfortable I find my bed here. I mentioned that I might start bringing my own bedding home with me from the flat. At the moment she is not keen to do anything, but I have left her thinking about it. If we leave it a while she may come round.'

'Thank you, Master Ted. I appreciate you trying for me.'

'I would suggest we wait until I am home for the summer and then raise the subject with her.'

Master Ted gave me a cheeky wink, not what I expected at all.

'I will do that. I appreciate you talking to her.' Hopefully progress was being made. The seed had been planted and all I had to do was wait for it to grow.

Before making an approach, once Master Ted was home for the summer, I thought it prudent to draw up a list of how many sheets, pillowcases, pillows, duvets and duvet covers would be needed. I then did some research around the costs of replacing all the bedding at once or by doing it in stages over the next few years. Either way the resulting totals were a bit eye-watering. I knew before I even thought about presenting the figures to Lady Linton that she would find any excuse not to spend that amount of money. She hated spending money on anything she thought wasn't absolutely essential to the running of Threldale, including decent bedding.

The number of beds I included was relatively high, but then Threldale was a big house. There were the large single beds in Lord and Lady Linton's separate bedroom suites, Master Ted's bedroom (a double), the Chinese bedroom (a double), the blue bedroom (a twin), the garden bedroom (a twin), the rose bedroom (a double) and the lilac bedroom (a twin). There were four other old servants' bedrooms that were hardly ever used, so I discounted them from my calculations. They could stay with sheets and blankets, and I would look at replacing the pillows on the beds in those rooms next year. That still added up to eight single duvets and three double duvets, never mind sheets, pillows and pillowcases.

Spring became summer and Master Ted returned home from university, complete with the bedding from his flat. With my ally at home I decided the time had come when I could put it off no longer. I needed to approach Lady Linton with my request and the costings. So one afternoon I cautiously entered the drawing room where I knew Lady Linton was taking coffee while she was reading a book, on what subject I couldn't quite discern. I took a deep breath and began.

'Lady Linton … Sorry to disturb you, but could I discuss something with you?'

'Of course, Rosie. My door is always open. I like to feel you can always discuss things with me. I will listen with an open mind, you know that.' She smiled at me, making me feel like a mouse being played with by a cat.

'I am having great difficulty keeping the sheets and blankets in good repair. I find that I have to apply patches to patches sometimes. And the pillows are all rather flat. I try to rotate them around so that at least your and Lord Linton's beds have the plumpest, but it is difficult. I think it may be time to look at some new bed linen.'

'I have noticed that the sheets on my bed have more than one repair to them, but does that really mean we need to buy new sheets?'

'Yes, Lady Linton. Some are now beyond my best efforts to repair. In fact, should we have a houseful of guests, I doubt I would be able to make up every bed with suitable sheets and pillow cases.'

'I didn't think it was that bad, though Teddy did mention something when he was home at Easter. Did you know that he has decided to use the bedding from his flat on his bed while he is home for the summer? I think Teddy might be right, and I may need to consider new bedding. However, I can't rush into this kind of expense. Let me think about it.'

That was progress on previous conversations on the subject, as it wasn't an outright dismissal of the proposal. I think that now he was home for the summer Master Ted must have continued nurturing the seed he had planted all those weeks ago at Easter, because it was only a few days after my conversation with her that Lady Linton asked to discuss bedding with me.

'Rosie, about the sheets that are beyond repair ... How many do we need to purchase?'

'I am sorry, Lady Linton, but we will need to consider pillowcases as well. Maybe even new pillows and – I know you are not happy with the idea, but duvets and duvet covers to replace the blankets.' I hoped I wasn't pushing my luck. I had my fingers crossed behind my back.

'Actually I have been giving this some thought myself. It may be that Lord Linton and I need to consider moving with the times regarding duvets and blankets. I will need some idea of how much this is all going to cost before I can even think of making any decisions. The finances of Threldale are not limitless.'

'I have already started looking at how much it will cost. I have broken it down into sheets, pillowcases, pillows, duvets and duvet covers. I have also been looking at replacing them over the next few years rather than all at once.' I handed over several sheets of paper with all my calculations on them.

'Now don't go thinking I have agreed to anything. I

need to look at these figures. I will let you know what I decide.' I thought that had gone rather well. Things were looking promising, but it still wasn't a done deal.

I left the Dining Room walking on air. I allowed myself to think about having a big bonfire of the smelly old pillows and cutting up the old bed linen to use as cleaning rags. I know Sam and Don were always looking for old rags for use in their workshop. I had plans to roll up the blankets and make them into draught excluders. Threldale was a very draughty place and Lady Linton would approve of my thriftiness.

Over the next few days I was itching to ask Lady Linton whether she was any closer to a decision, but knew better than to voice my impatience. She might dig her heels in or completely change her mind if she thought I was pushing her towards extravagant spending.

The days lengthened into weeks. Master Ted returned to university, taking his bedding with him after the long summer break. The nights began to close in, but there was still no word. I was beginning to think Lady Linton was avoiding the issue. I needed to hold my nerve and wait.

One frosty morning in early October the front door bell went and I opened the door to a delivery van with a man unloading several very large packages on to the gravel drive. He was whistling something tuneless as he unloaded the parcels.

'Morning, love. Got a delivery for a Lady Linton. Where shall I put them?' He smiled at me.

'Leave them next to the table in the hall, please.' A pet hate of mine is being called 'love' by people I don't know, but I let it pass. He picked the packages up one at a time and brought them into the Entrance Hall, and after adding the last one to the pile he turned to me.

'Right, sign here and I'll be off. Ta.' I signed where he pointed. He turned around, left the house, jumped into his van and drove off.

As far as I was concerned there were no deliveries expected, so I had no idea what the packages were. I would have to wait until Lady Linton appeared. It had to be something she had ordered, but she had neglected to tell me to expect a delivery.

When Lady Linton arrived down for breakfast she knew exactly what the packages were and, yes, she had been expecting them.

'Rosie, that is the new bedding. I ordered it a few days ago by telephone from Leeds. Sort it out, will you? And make up my and Lord Linton's beds with the new duvets. We'll see how we get on with them tonight.'

'Yes, Lady Linton.' So it was new bedding, but what had Lady Linton ordered? How much had she ordered? I was quite excited to unpack the boxes find out. It felt like Christmas had come early.

I took the packages from the Entrance Hall through to the laundry room and began unpacking it all. By the time I had unpacked everything I had one pile of cardboard, paper and plastic and another pile of factory-stiff new bed linen. I placed the various items in piles, counting as I went, and was stunned to see that my full list was all here before me: sheets, pillowcases, pillows, duvets and duvet covers. She had ordered white Egyptian cotton sheets and pillowcases. The duvet covers were white too but had a pattern of silk stripes on them. Very sophisticated. I could hardly believe Lady Linton had ordered everything I had asked for. Now I had the huge job of getting it all washed and ironed ready for putting on the beds, starting with Lord and Lady Linton's single beds.

By the end of the day I had most of it washed, dried and ironed. I had stripped the old bedding off the two single beds in their bedroom suites and put the new bedding on, including replacing the old blankets and pillows with the new duvets and pillows. Now I had to wait and see whether they would take to the idea of sleeping under a duvet with a big fluffy pillow under their head or want their old threadbare sheets, blankets and flat, smelly pillows back.

The next morning I waited with some trepidation for Lord and Lady Linton to come down to breakfast. Lord Linton was the first to appear in the Dining Room, and before I could make a tentative enquiry about how he had slept he offered his own opinion on the new bedding.

'Rosie, there are no blankets on my bed. Instead there's a sort of quilt thing. Wasn't sure about it, but slept like a log. Is that big quilt one of those modern duvet things?'

'Yes, Lord Linton.'

'Marvellous. Should have changed from blankets years ago. Never knew it would be so light and comfortable. I was warm as toast. Well done!'

'Thank you.'

'The pillow seemed sort of bigger and fluffier. Was that new too?'

'Yes, Lord Linton.'

'Jolly good. I feel ready for a good breakfast now.' I hoped Lady Linton's reaction would be as positive.

Lady Linton came down twenty minutes later looking a little bleary-eyed and tired. I was not hopeful of a good reaction to the new bedding.

'Rosie, that was the worst night's sleep I have ever had. Get that duvet off my bed and put the blankets back on. How is anyone supposed to sleep under something that has no weight to it?' She was tired, and when she was tired she was not happy. 'The new pillows are fine. They can stay on my bed. I didn't realise the old pillows were so thin, but that duvet thing is most uncomfortable. How is one supposed to keep it on the bed? I tossed and turned all night and didn't sleep a wink.'

'No, Lady Linton.'

'It doesn't even tuck in. How anyone manages to sleep under something that doesn't stay in place on the bed I have no idea.'

'Yes, Lady Linton.' I was more than a little disappointed that she was not going to give it more than a single night before dismissing it. There was no point me trying to persuade her, as that would just make her dig her heels in.

Later that day I took the nice new sweet-smelling duvet off her bed and replaced it with the old threadbare blankets. I left the new pillows and linen on her bed, as she had requested. I bagged up the duvet and put it away in the linen cupboard, hoping that some day in the future Lady Linton would try again to get on with a duvet instead of blankets. At least Lord Linton was happy with the new duvet and I didn't have to swap his bedding back.

When Lady Linton came down the following morning after a night back under the smelly old blankets she still looked bleary-eyed, tired and, if it was possible, even more short-tempered.

'Rosie, I had another awful night. The blankets felt so heavy, and I have never noticed that before. What is even more disturbing is that they smell musty. This really can't go on. I need my sleep. Take the blankets off and put the duvet back on. I will have to give it another try, much against my better judgement. I really cannot have another sleepless night. I am beginning to wish I had never agreed to this whole idea of duvets.' She was almost barking at me.

'Yes, Lady Linton.' I headed up to her bedroom suite straight away and took the horrible old blankets off. I retrieved the duvet from the linen cupboard, popped a cover on it and put it back on the bed. I hoped this would be the last time I would ever need to put blankets on her bed.

The next morning I almost dreaded Lady Linton coming down to breakfast. Would she have finally had a good night's sleep? Would I have to change over the bedding yet again? I hovered in the vicinity of the Dining Room, waiting for her to appear. When she did she still looked bleary-eyed. I wasn't hopeful.

'I slept a little better last night. I do believe I got at least a couple of hours. I may be able to get used to the duvet, given time. We shall keep it on for now but if I don't adjust to it over the next week or so then we may have to invest in new blankets.' She headed in for breakfast. As far as I was concerned that was a positive reaction, and one I was happy to go with.

I spent the next couple of days working my way around the other beds I had earmarked for modernising, taking off all the old bedding and replacing it with new pillows, pillowcases, sheets, duvets and duvet covers. They looked so much better, as well as smelling better. As far as I was concerned the beds were now fit for guests to use. I would no longer be embarrassed at having guests sleeping under patched sheets, smelly blankets and flat pillows.

As for my plans for the old bedding … I waited a few weeks to be sure that Lady Linton did not ask for them to be put on any of the beds. Then one day, when Lord and Lady Linton were both out for the day, and with help from the gardeners, we made a big bonfire of the old pillows. The smell that came off the old feathers as they burnt was awful, but it was worth it to see them finally destroyed.

The blankets were washed, dried, rolled up and stitched into door-length sausages. I found some old curtains in a cupboard and used them to make removable covers for the draught excluders. This took me a few weeks to do, working in the evenings, and once I had completed them I placed them in front of the doors to the bedrooms, the reception rooms and also in my own little flat.

The sheets were ripped up into piles of rags. I kept half for use inside Threldale when I was spring-cleaning, and Sam and Don took the other half. They were always short of rags. I am not sure what they used them for but they were grateful to receive them.

Lady Linton didn't mention blankets – old or new – again, and I never did have to remove the duvet from her bed. A satisfactory result all round.

Lightning Source UK Ltd.
Milton Keynes UK
UKHW040631280419
341730UK00001B/5/P